A Sharp Character

He came at Slocum again. This time, he made a quick feinting stab to draw Slocum's arms down before taking a quick swing at shoulder level. The blade sliced through a good section of meat, spraying Slocum's blood onto the ground. Just as he was recovering from that, Slocum saw the man lunge in for another stab.

Slocum was barely quick enough to cross his arms at the wrists and drop them down to divert the blade before it was buried hilt-deep into his gut. He then twisted to one side and closed his hands around the man's wrist like a set of pincers. A sharp twist and forceful grab allowed him to relieve the man of his weapon. Slocum spun around to face him, finding nothing but empty space. Suddenly, an arm snaked around his neck from behind and a fist pounded against his ribs.

"How do you like that?" the man snarled into Slocum's ear. "Not so good, is it? Well, it's about to get a whole lot worse."

DON'T MISS THESE
ALL-ACTION WESTERN SERIES
FROM THE BERKLEY PUBLISHING GROUP

THE GUNSMITH by J. R. Roberts
Clint Adams was a legend among lawmen, outlaws, and ladies. They called him . . . the Gunsmith.

LONGARM by Tabor Evans
The popular long-running series about Deputy U.S. Marshal Custis Long—his life, his loves, his fight for justice.

SLOCUM by Jake Logan
Today's longest-running action Western. John Slocum rides a deadly trail of hot blood and cold steel.

BUSHWHACKERS by B. J. Lanagan
An action-packed series by the creators of Longarm! The rousing adventures of the most brutal gang of cutthroats ever assembled—Quantrill's Raiders.

DIAMONDBACK by Guy Brewer
Dex Yancey is Diamondback, a Southern gentleman turned con man when his brother cheats him out of the family fortune. Ladies love him. Gamblers hate him. But nobody pulls one over on Dex . . .

WILDGUN by Jack Hanson
The blazing adventures of mountain man Will Barlow— from the creators of Longarm!

TEXAS TRACKER by Tom Calhoun
J.T. Law: the most relentless—and dangerous—manhunter in all Texas. Where sheriffs and posses fail, he's the best man to bring in the most vicious outlaws—for a price.

JAKE LOGAN

SLOCUM
AND THE
YELLOWBACK TRAIL

J

JOVE BOOKS, NEW YORK

THE BERKLEY PUBLISHING GROUP
Published by the Penguin Group
Penguin Group (USA) Inc.
375 Hudson Street, New York, New York 10014, USA
Penguin Group (Canada), 90 Eglinton Avenue East, Suite 700, Toronto, Ontario M4P 2Y3, Canada
(a division of Pearson Penguin Canada Inc.)
Penguin Books Ltd., 80 Strand, London WC2R 0RL, England
Penguin Group Ireland, 25 St. Stephen's Green, Dublin 2, Ireland (a division of Penguin Books Ltd.)
Penguin Group (Australia), 250 Camberwell Road, Camberwell, Victoria 3124, Australia
(a division of Pearson Australia Group Pty. Ltd.)
Penguin Books India Pvt. Ltd., 11 Community Centre, Panchsheel Park, New Delhi—110 017, India
Penguin Group (NZ), 67 Apollo Drive, Rosedale, North Shore 0632, New Zealand
(a division of Pearson New Zealand Ltd.)
Penguin Books (South Africa) (Pty.) Ltd., 24 Sturdee Avenue, Rosebank, Johannesburg 2196,
South Africa

Penguin Books Ltd., Registered Offices: 80 Strand, London WC2R 0RL, England

This is a work of fiction. Names, characters, places, and incidents either are the product of the author's imagination or are used fictitiously, and any resemblance to actual persons, living or dead, business establishments, events, or locales is entirely coincidental.

SLOCUM AND THE YELLOWBACK TRAIL

A Jove Book / published by arrangement with the author

PRINTING HISTORY
Jove edition / September 2010

Copyright © 2010 by Penguin Group (USA) Inc.
Cover illustration by Sergio Giovine.

ISBN: 978-0-515-14838-1

JOVE®
Jove Books are published by The Berkley Publishing Group,
a division of Penguin Group (USA) Inc.
375 Hudson Street, New York, New York 10014.
JOVE® is a registered trademark of Penguin Group (USA) Inc.
The "J" design is a trademark of Penguin Group (USA) Inc.

PRINTED IN THE UNITED STATES OF AMERICA

10 9 8 7 6 5 4 3 2 1

1

CHICAGO, ILLINOIS

The Stamper Theater was in a section of Chicago that still smelled like wood that had been burned during the Great Fire. Chicago already had a very distinctive scent to it, and the scorched remnants of that tragedy didn't help matters. The fire had been put out long ago, but Chicago wasn't the sort of place to sit still. There had been plenty more going on since, from labor disputes to common street fights. Somehow the buildings on the corner across from the theater hadn't been burned in the famous fire at all. There was more than enough friction in Chicago to spark any number of infernos.

It had been a while since Slocum had visited that town. Most of the time, he preferred more wide open spaces and sweeter scents in the air. Chicago did have a certain appeal which drew all sorts of folks to its streets. There were plenty of exotic foods to eat, goods to buy, and sights to see. That was all well and good, but it took a bit more to bring Slocum all the way into Illinois. To be exact, it took seven hundred and fifty dollars.

That was the amount of money Terrance Pinder was offering Slocum to deal with a certain infestation plaguing his place of business. Slocum had met Terrance when the Stamper Theater still smelled of freshly cut lumber and wet paint. It had been a chance encounter facilitated by one of the prettiest faces in town. Terrance's daughter Eve wasn't as immediately attractive as some of the girls working at the Stamper, but the light inside of her shone brightly enough to make her rise above the rest. Like most every man in town, Slocum had been drawn to her. And, like all those other men, he had been chased off by her father. But while the rest of Eve's would-be suitors found other pastures to graze in, Slocum remained for a while.

In all the time that had passed, Slocum nearly forgot about the Stamper Theater. He hadn't forgotten about Eve, however, and assumed hers was the elegant handwriting on the envelope that had been delivered to him while he was staying in Missouri. It wasn't. The script was Terrance's, as was the offer to return to Chicago for what promised to be a very lucrative job. Seven hundred and fifty dollars was just too tempting to pass up, so Slocum bought a train ticket to the Windy City.

The Stamper Theater was a large box of a building near the corner of Twelfth and Halstead. It was close enough to the tracks to hear trains rattle by, but not so close that the iron horses drowned out the rambunctious cries of the theater's more energetic patrons. There were better places to build a theater, but it seemed the location was the least of its owner's problems.

Slocum walked in through a set of double doors which opened into a room that took up most of the building's first floor. There was a bar to his right, stretching from the front of the room to about a quarter of the way back. To the left of the entrance, several gambling tables were set up against the wall. Games included roulette and faro, but they weren't the only ones being played. Several of the tables scattered throughout the front half of the room were hosting privately run card games. Most of the back half of the room was taken up by a stage. The velvet curtain had seen better days, but the girls dancing in front of it were in decent enough shape. Before he could get a better look at his surroundings, Slocum was nearly bowled over by a man who reeked of cheap pipe tobacco.

"John Slocum!" Terrance Pinder said. "I was starting to think you weren't going to show up."

"It's been less than a week since I got the letter," Slocum pointed out. "How fast did you expect me to move?"

Terrance was in his late forties, but he had enough wrinkles to tack on another decade to his appearance, although his blue eyes were bright and alert. His thinning hair was hastily pressed down onto his scalp, making it seem as if all of his effort in grooming had been spent in maintaining the intricate mustache that connected one sideburn to the other. Those sideburns nearly covered his ears and cheeks, but paled in comparison to the trail of whiskers that headed toward the edges of his mouth before veering north to run beneath his nose. Where most men might scratch their head or chin while thinking, he brushed the side of his finger against his mustache and traced it all the way to an overgrown sideburn. "Has it only been a week? Seems like a lot longer than that."

"Looks like the theater is doing well. Is Eve still around?"

"She's here somewhere. Would you like a drink?"

"What I'd like is to know what's so important that you went through the trouble of tracking me down. Come to think of it," Slocum added, "how'd you manage that?"

Terrance clasped his hands behind his back and rocked back and forth upon his heels. When he spoke this time, the English accent he'd brought with him from the east end of London was just as fresh as the day he'd stepped off the boat. "It was quite a feat, but I managed it. Of course, as they say, where there's a will there's a way."

Since he'd been led to the bar, Slocum asked the tender for a whiskey and then shifted his focus back to Terrance. "You still haven't told me how you tracked me down."

"Does it matter?"

Considering how many dangerous men would like to know where to find him, Slocum had become uneasy with the fact that some theater owner could set his sights on him. "Yeah. It matters."

Terrance tugged at his collar and nervously cleared his throat before replying, "I've made the acquaintance of several saloon owners in Illinois and Missouri. One of them told me about a man who'd shot the place up after some argument over a card game and your name came up."

Some of the uneasiness in Slocum's belly faded when he heard that. "Ah, yes. That would have been the poker tournament in Jefferson City."

"No, it was an all-night game in Hannibal."

"I suppose that one did get pretty rough too."

"Rough enough for a friend of mine to mention your name when he came to pay me a visit," Terrance said. "He said you took one of his best dancers along when leaving town, which told me we were discussing the same John Slocum. He knew where you were headed, so I sent you that letter. Hope you don't mind."

Lifting his whiskey glass, Slocum asked, "So what's the seven-hundred-and-fifty-dollar problem?"

Terrance turned so he could lean with his back against the bar and then nodded toward the roulette wheel on the opposite side of the room. "See the man spinning that wheel?"

Picking the fellow out in less than a second, Slocum grunted, "Yeah."

"Here's an advance," Terrance said as he slapped four hundred dollars onto the bar. "Setting that one up for a fall will be enough to earn that much."

2

Slocum ambled across the room, sipping from his whiskey while weaving between the card tables. It was early enough in the day for him to make the trip without being jostled too often, but there was still enough of a crowd to keep him from sticking out like a sore thumb. Along the way, he watched the small group of men clustered around the wheel. The first thing he noticed was the absence of working girls in that vicinity. Considering how much money was surely being tossed about by the gamblers, that spoke volumes. Working girls made a living by getting close to men who were willing to spend their money. As far as Slocum was concerned, nobody was more willing to spend money than someone who wagered on where a little ball would land in a slotted wheel. Before he even made it to the wheel, he got a real good idea of what kept the theater's ladies from getting too close.

"If you want that hand back, mister, I'd suggest you take it away from that cash."

The one who made the threat was a tall, skinny fellow who stood behind the wheel. He wore a blue silk shirt with dark sweat stains under both arms and across his chest. Although it was a bit warm for September, this man appeared to be suffering most for it. None of the sweat made it to his face, which was sunken and covered in scars that crossed his cheeks like paths traced on a map.

Standing across from him at the table was a young man dressed in a stained white shirt. Since some of those stains had the look of dried blood, Slocum guessed the man either got into a lot of fights or worked at one of the nearby slaughterhouses. He stretched one arm out to a stack of cash on the edge of the table closest to the skinny fellow. Even though he glanced back and forth at the men around him, he wasn't quick to retract his hand. "I won that spin," he said. "It landed on eight. See for yourself."

"I can see just fine," the skinny man snapped. "That's how I can see you bet on nine."

"I bet on both of 'em."

"So you say now that it landed on eight."

By now, Slocum was close enough to get a better look at the table itself. Not only was the paint so faded that it was difficult to discern one number from another, but the chips were scattered so haphazardly that they might as well have been thrown down from the ceiling. One or two of the other gamblers at that table must have been friends of the one in the bloody shirt, because he pulled himself up and made another reach for the money. "I set my bet down on the line between eight and nine, so I'm owed some money. Hand it over or I'll take it."

Stretching his neck out like a snake lunging for a carelessly placed foot, the man behind the wheel dropped his left hand down onto the young fellow's wrist and snarled, "You won't take nothin', boy." His right hand rose up from where it had been tucked beneath the table to reveal a wicked-looking stiletto. "And if you make another move for my money, I'll add that hand of yours to my collection."

"What's the problem here?" Slocum asked as he shoved

between two of the men who watched the brewing fight instead of the dance being performed by the girls on stage.

Without moving either hand, the man behind the wheel said, "Next spin is comin'. First I gotta teach this here boy some manners."

Sure enough, two of the other gamblers were friends of the younger fellow, because they closed ranks around him. Before they could do much to help their companion, they were grabbed by sets of hands that came so quickly from behind that they even took Slocum by surprise. They weren't stealthy so much as brash enough to storm up and take hold of the gamblers as if they had every right to do so. The men who'd grabbed the gamblers pulled them away like fishermen dragging trout from a stream. Whatever protests the gamblers made were quickly silenced by a few well-placed fists.

Although Slocum didn't enjoy watching men get beaten just for coming to the aid of a friend, it was a bit late to do anything about it now. The punches stopped as suddenly as they'd started. The stiletto, on the other hand, was still very much in play over the roulette table.

"All right, Bo," the young man said. He pulled his hand away from the cash stacked near the wheel, but his eyes remained fixed upon the other man's knife. "No need to make this worse. You can keep your money."

"Really?" Bo sneered in a way that made his sunken face twist into a hungry grin. "How very kind of you."

When the young man attempted to move his hand, the stiletto twitched down just far enough to scrape sharpened steel on flesh. "I said keep your damn money!"

Bo shook his head. "This ain't about the money no more. It's about setting an example. Folks need to know they can't just strut up to my game and do whatever they like."

Since the young man's friends had been dispatched, the two who'd pulled them away stalked toward the table. Any of the others who'd wanted to leave decided to stay put just to keep from being noticed. As Bo raised his stiletto another inch or so while tightening his grip, most of the gamblers within eyeshot watched with morbid fascination, in anticipation of the bloody display that was about to be shown to them.

Bo watched expectantly also. In addition to the anticipation shared by his audience, his eyes glittered with something else that could only be found in the cruelest of animals. Blood was going to be spilled and he meant to enjoy every last second of it.

The rest of the theater went about its business, unaware of or just plain accustomed to what was happening at the roulette wheel. When Bo's arm tensed and he started to lean forward, everyone in the immediate vicinity held his breath.

Everyone but Slocum, that is.

The instant Bo flexed a muscle to drive his blade down into the table through the young man's hand, Slocum drew his pistol. The Colt Navy came up in a whisper of iron against leather. His arm moved in a practiced motion that put the gun in his hand and its barrel against Bo's wrist.

At first, Bo was annoyed to have his progress stopped by an immovable barrier. When he saw that barrier was the business end of a six-shooter, he let his eyes follow the gun back up to the man holding it. "What the hell's this?" he grunted. "You a friend of this cheat?"

"Never met him."

"Then why would you risk your life to protect him?"

Since Slocum could feel any movement of Bo's hand through the Colt's grip, he allowed his eyes to shift just enough to get a look at the figures encroaching on him from the side. Before Bo could get any smart ideas, Slocum said, "Maybe it's easier to believe his story than the words coming from the mouth of a skinny little rat like yourself."

"That's a dangerous play, mister."

"It sure is. If either of your boys gets any closer to me, I'm liable to get nervous. If I get nervous, my finger may just twitch. And if that happens, this young fella won't be the one missing a paw."

Bo's arm started to tremble. Whether it was from nervousness or fatigue was tough to tell.

"Fine," Bo said as he eased his arm back and let go of the young man's wrist.

"Very fine indeed," Slocum said. "Now pay the man what you owe him."

Bo's eyes narrowed as he slowly moved back. "Pay him for cheating?"

Nudging the young gambler with the side of his foot, Slocum asked, "Did you cheat?"

"No sir," the gambler replied.

Slocum grinned. "Somehow, I believe him more than you, Bo. Why don't you pay up like a proper dealer so you can get on with your game?"

The expression on Bo's sunken face made him look as if he'd just been forced to drink a bucket of sour milk. He grabbed a stack of money, peeled off a few bills, and threw them at the gambler. "Take it and get the hell out of my sight. Come near my table again and I'll finish what I started here today."

"Don't worry," the gambler said while collecting his money. "There's plenty more games to be played around here." To Slocum, he said, "Much obliged, mister."

Bo's men moved behind Slocum. He took a quick glance over one shoulder, spotted one of the big fellows coming at him, and snapped his arm around like a whip. The Colt Navy cracked against the side of that man's head and dropped him to the floor.

Slocum then took aim at the other fellow while stepping away from the table. "This is over as far as I'm concerned," he warned. "If you want to press the matter, it's your call."

"Ain't nothing's over, mister," Bo replied. "Not unless you repay me here and now."

"That's not gonna happen."

"Care to tell me your name?"

"Nah," Slocum said. "I'm through with you. If you boys keep your noses clean, it'll stay that way." With that, he holstered his Colt and tipped his hat to all three men. The one who'd been knocked in the head was shaky on his feet and bleeding, but not seriously damaged.

Since nobody else was eager to test him, Slocum made his way back to where Terrance was standing. "That was fun," he said to the theater's owner. "How about another whiskey?"

Terrance shook his head and wiped a few beads of sweat from his brow. "I can't believe you did that."

"What were you expecting?"

"I wanted you to get those men out of my theater for good, not stir them up like a damned hornet's nest! You think this is through?"

Watching Bo and his two partners collect themselves before quietly getting their table back in order, Slocum shrugged. "Seems to be doing pretty well at the moment."

As if to prove Slocum's point, the rattle of the ball in the roulette wheel soon came from that side of the room. Within moments, it was followed by the voices of gamblers placing their bets and howling for their numbers. "You don't know those men," Terrance muttered. "They won't let this go. If anything, it'll just be worse next time."

"Well that's next time. Right now, I'd like the rest of my money."

When Terrance fixed him with a set of wide eyes above a gaping mouth, Slocum had to fight to keep from laughing. He gave in before Terrance busted a seam in his shirt. "I'm just pulling your leg, Terrance. Take a breath, will you?"

"Wish I could."

"Who'd you say those boys are again?"

"Bo's the one behind the wheel," Terrance replied. "His

partners are James and Cam. James is the one you knocked in the head. He runs girls through the rooms of my second floor, and he won't be at all happy once he gets his wits about him."

"He doesn't look happy now," Slocum chuckled.

"I'm glad you find this so funny!" Terrance said while moving closer to the bar. "You can just pick up and leave if things get bad enough. I've got a business to run. A business, I might add, that may get burned to the ground thanks to you. Bo threatened to do that, you know! Why the hell do you think I need your help with this?"

Slocum lifted his drink to his mouth and tossed it back. The firewater burned all the way down his throat and left him willing to grin about the situation. "This," he said while setting the glass onto the bar, "is some damn fine whiskey. As for the rest, I may not know those men personally but I've dealt with their kind more times than I can count. They're full of wind and enjoy pushing folks that they think won't push back."

The first ray of hope showed on Terrance's face when he asked, "So you think they really won't set my place on fire?"

"Oh, they still might do that. That'd be just the sort of thing I'd expect from a bunch of cowards like that."

Terrance's hopes fell right through the floor along with his chin.

"But," Slocum continued, "I don't intend on letting it get that far. They'll set their sights on me for now. After what I did to Bo, they'll want to put me in my place before burning down their source of income."

"And what should I do when you're not around?" Raising one eyebrow expectantly, he added, "Unless you don't plan on leaving?"

"I'll come and go like anyone else," Slocum said while patting the other man's shoulder. "And when they strut up to try and talk tough to you, just do whatever you'd normally do to keep them quiet. Leave the rest to me."

"So you'll clean them out? Permanently?"

"I'll do the job you're paying me to do and don't worry. When I leave town, you won't have to concern yourself with those fellas again. There is still a payment coming, though, right?"

"Sure. Once the job's done. If there's any damage to my place, I'll have to deduct it from your fee."

Slocum studied Terrance with a harsh eye. Seeing the other man was going to stand his ground, he nodded and asked, "Do you provide free drinks to your employees?"

"No, but I'll make an exception for you."

"Then you've got a deal. So, where's your daughter?"

Whatever nervousness Terrance may have felt before was quickly replaced by a ferocious resolve that showed from the glint of his eye all the way down to the straightening of his spine. "Eve's got her own matters to tend to and so do you. Your only concern with her is if Bo or those hired guns of his go anywhere near her. Understand?"

"Yes, sir," Slocum replied with a mock salute. Even though the older man's hackles were still up, Slocum told him, "You're a good fellow, Terrance. I'll see about cleaning out this theater for you. I won't accept a dime until then."

"And what about Eve?"

"What about her?"

Straightening up even more, Terrance placed one hand flat upon the bar and the other upon his hip. "You'll give her a wide berth?"

"I'm not here to hide. If she catches sight of me and waves, it'd be rude not to wave back."

"Waving isn't what I meant."

"She's a grown woman, Terrance. She'll do what she pleases. If it'll make you feel better, I won't go out hunting for her."

"That does make me feel better, John. Thank you." Slapping the bar, Terrance caught the tender's eye and said, "Anything this man wants to drink is on the house!"

"You're a good man," Slocum said.

"You too," Terrance replied with a relieved sigh. "Welcome to Chicago."

3

"God," Eve Pinder moaned, "it's so good to have you in Chicago."

Slocum sat on a chair that creaked under his weight. Actually, it creaked under the combined weight of both him and Eve. She was a short, solidly built woman with curves in all the right places and a thick mane of black hair extending just past her shoulders. Her breasts were just big enough to sway as she straddled him and just small enough to keep her nipples at Slocum's mouth level as she ground on his lap.

"That," he replied after taking a playful bite of her left breast, "is just what I was gonna say to you."

Eve smiled and leaned back while grabbing onto the back of the chair. Her face was just as pretty as Slocum remembered. What struck him the most was the little gap between her top front teeth that made her look even prettier and more genuine than a dancing girl who'd spent hours gussying herself up with the war paint they used before going on stage. In contrast to those women, Eve barely seemed to give a damn what anyone thought of her. She straddled

Slocum and rode his cock as if she was breaking a bronco. Looking down at him, she reached around to grasp the back of his head and press his mouth against her nipple even harder. When his teeth closed around her flesh, she twitched and let out a happy little yelp.

"When my daddy told me to stay away from the theater, I knew something good was going on," she said.

Slocum grabbed her hips and leaned back just enough to get some breathing room. "I was hoping as much. Your father runs a nice place, but I didn't want to stand about all night long."

"How long were you waiting for me?"

"Just over two hours. Can't say I was bored, though."

Settling on him so Slocum's erection was buried deep inside of her, Eve let out a slow breath and moved her hand to his chest. She ran the other flat along her belly until her fingertips drifted into the thatch of hair between her legs. "Don't tell me you were letting one of those dancing girls entertain you."

"No. The roulette spinner kept me entertained well enough."

"You and Bo? Now, that is a surprise. I wouldn't have pegged you as that sort of man."

Slocum gritted his teeth and made a snarling sound as he grabbed onto Eve's rump and lifted her up along with him as he stood up from the chair. "You know damn well that isn't what I mean."

"Maybe you're getting bored with women," she said teasingly. Although she started to needle him some more, her words were cut off when she was unceremoniously dropped onto the bed. She landed on her back and barely had a chance to scoot so her backside wasn't dangling off the edge of the mattress before Slocum was easing her legs apart.

"Does this look bored to you?" he asked while guiding his rigid pole into her pussy and thrusting his hips forward.

Eve's eyes widened and she pulled in a quick breath.

Her imperfect smile returned. This time, it carried a devilish glimmer. Reaching down again, she touched herself and eased her fingers apart so Slocum's cock was sliding between them while he entered her. "Doesn't feel bored, that's for certain. Oooh! Feels even less bored now."

Being inside of her felt good enough, but feeling her touch his erect penis as he slid in and out was even better. She knew full well what she was doing to him, because Eve kept her eyes focused on him as she moved her fingers up and down his length.

"So you know Bo?" Slocum asked as a way to distract himself so he wouldn't end his tussle with her ahead of schedule.

"He's just some tough-talking idiot who pushes gamblers around."

"Did he ever try his luck with you?"

"Why? Do you think he'd know how to curl my toes?"

Slocum chuckled and pulled out of her. "No, but I do." With that, he gave her hip a little slap and rolled her over. Eve was more than happy to comply and crawled onto the bed so she was on all fours with her knees on the edge and her feet dangling off the side. Slocum ran the palms of his hands along the curve of her backside and up to the small of her back. Before she could get too anxious, he moved forward so his erection brushed the dampness between her thighs. Already impatient, Eve reached down to guide him the rest of the way.

The instant he felt the warm wetness close in around him, Slocum buried his pole as far into her as it would go. He grabbed her hips and pulled her toward him just to add that little bit of impact when his stomach bumped against her. Eve clawed at the bed like a cat and arched her back as he continued to drive into her. Before long, a groan emerged from her throat and came out in a prolonged cry. Her entire body shook as a climax rippled through it, but she wasn't done with him yet.

"I heard my father hired you to lay down the law at the Stamper," she said. "What would you do if I tried to start some trouble?"

"I'd have to put you in your place." Knowing she was smiling without having to see her face, Slocum pounded into her again and again. Her pussy was dripping and the pleasure she felt was so intense that she could hardly make a sound for the next couple of minutes. When he felt another set of shivers work through her, Slocum eased out and gave her rump another little slap.

Eve rolled onto her side and stretched out on the bed. "Bo's not the one you should be worried about," she told him as he settled onto the bed next to her. "James is the killer of that bunch."

"What about the other one? Younger fella with light-colored hair."

"That's Cam. He used to be a deputy. My guess is that he took a few bribes and got in over his head with the wrong sort of people. He'll do what the other two tell him, but not if it means getting himself killed."

"How do you know so much?"

"I see a lot of things," she replied as she let her eyes wander along the front of Slocum's naked body.

Slocum's eyes were doing some wandering of their own, and they settled upon the smooth skin between her breasts. Eve's body had the texture of warm cream, and there wasn't a single part of her that wasn't pleasant to the touch. Although plenty of women had soft skin, Eve made no attempt to hide the fact that she enjoyed putting hers on display. Just seeing him look at her was enough for her to stretch her arms out and move her legs apart to give Slocum a better view.

"Does my father know I'm here?" she asked.

"I didn't tell him I was renting a room in this particular establishment, but he must have seen you run up and plant that kiss on me when you stopped by the theater. If it's all the same to you, I wouldn't mind dropping the subject of your father for the moment."

"Why?" she asked while reaching down to wrap her fingers around his cock. "Does that make things hard for you?"

"Not really."

"I beg to differ," she said while stroking him back to a mostly rigid state. "The only reason I asked about him was because he tends to check up on me whenever I'm not at home or in his sight."

"He hired me to protect his interests," Slocum said.

"I don't think that makes us entirely safe from him, especially after he caught us in the back room at his own theater the last time you were in town."

"Almost caught us," he corrected. "As far as he knows we were just kissing like a couple of randy kids."

"That's enough for him to get suspicious. If he knew about the rest of it," she added while draping one leg over him and shifting so his cock brushed against the slick lips of her pussy, "there'd be hell to pay."

"All right," Slocum said. "Enough talk about your father or anything else." He grabbed the leg that had been resting across his hip and held it so he could have an easier time getting inside of her. It took some shifting, but they were soon lying on their sides facing each other. Slocum held her leg in place and began thrusting his hips.

It wasn't long before that became more awkward than it was worth. When he rolled her onto her back, she spread her legs open wide as he knelt between them. From there, it was a simple matter of plunging his cock into her and pumping in and out with building momentum. Eve drove her head back against the bed and grabbed onto the blankets with both hands. As soon as she felt Slocum's hands reaching to cup her buttocks, she pumped her hips in time with his.

Her reckless abandon drove her over the edge almost immediately and would have done the same for Slocum if he hadn't reined himself in with a few gulping breaths. She felt too damn good for him to be through just yet. Even if she'd wait to stoke his fire again later, he just couldn't finish with her yet. Fortunately, the tide within him eased back and he was free to do as he pleased once more.

Slocum ran his hands along her inner thighs, rubbed her calves, and finally grabbed her ankles. The devilish grin reappeared on her face as she hoisted her feet up and allowed him to move them apart. The moment Slocum let go, she wrapped her legs around him and ground herself against his stiff member.

Judging by the sheen of sweat on her skin and the fatigue written on her face, Eve was spent. Trembling orgasms had shaken her several times, but now she could barely lift her head. That meant it was Slocum's time to cut loose. He pumped into her however he pleased while Eve simply enjoyed the ride.

"Yes," she moaned as he pounded into her again and again. When Slocum grabbed her tits with both hands, she pressed her hands upon his and arched her back. "God yes! Right there!"

Somehow, she was going to climax again. Slocum envied her for being able to take so much pleasure from a single tussle. Then again, he doubted he'd be able to survive more than one at a stretch of what was brewing inside of him. The sensations rolled through him and he did nothing to push them back. He simply allowed his hands to roam over her silky skin and his hips to pump between her legs like a piston. When the explosion came, he wrapped his arms around her and drove his cock in as far as it could go.

"I don't . . . don't know how you do it," she gasped. "But I'm sure as hell glad you did."

When Slocum's eyesight cleared, he looked around at the room he'd rented. Clothes were strewn across the floor and the sparse furnishings. Both chairs were set at strange angles from where they'd started. The curtains had been nearly pulled from their rod in Eve's haste to draw them, and then there was the bed. Not only were the linens a rumpled mess, but the frame had shifted to another spot somewhere during all the vigorous activity in the last few minutes.

"Damn," he huffed as he rolled onto his back. "Maybe I should have picked a hotel a little farther away from the Stamper."

"You afraid my father might hear me scream and come to my rescue?"

"Wouldn't want him too sore at me," Slocum said. "He went through a lot of trouble to bring me in as a hired gun."

"The John Slocum I know isn't a hired gun." As she shifted onto her other side, Eve pulled the blanket up along with her. While the material covered her somewhat, she obviously wasn't too concerned about the rest. "So you came back to take care of Bo?"

"That was the idea."

"I thought you just came for me."

"Well you didn't really give me a chance to explain myself," Slocum replied. "One minute I was standing at your father's bar and the next you were dragging me outside."

"You told me you'd been standing around for a few hours," she reminded him.

"It all just ran together," he groaned. "Bo packed up his game and left not long after I introduced myself to him and after that, there wasn't much else besides the stage show to hold my attention."

Eve allowed the blanket to fall away from her breasts as she tossed her hair over one shoulder and said, "And then I came along. Aren't you the lucky boy?"

"So what do you know about Bo and those men at the roulette wheel?"

At first, Eve seemed confused. Then, she seemed mildly irritated as she scooted even closer to him and asked, "You really want to ask me about that now?"

"I wanted to ask you about it when I first saw you, but didn't get a chance."

"You could've said anything you wanted," she griped. "You're a grown man. Lord knows I wouldn't want to distract you from whatever else you'd rather be doing."

Slocum rubbed her shoulder and then allowed his hand to graze her chest. "What can I say? No man can resist some temptations."

While she may have known he was sweetening her up a bit, Eve appreciated the effort. "You'd best watch yourself, John Slocum."

"I'd rather watch you."

No matter the motive behind those words, they did the trick just fine. "Bo's been in Chicago for a year. He thinks he's a bad man, but couldn't harm a fly without help from James. All he cares about is making easy money and he's more than happy to push around the fools that take a chance on that spinning wheel of his. Cam joined up with them a few months ago. His heart's in the right place, but he was led astray."

"Aww," Slocum said with plenty of sarcasm in his tone. "Ain't that just tragic."

"Do you want to hear this or not?"

"Go ahead."

After a few more seconds of glaring at him, Eve went on. "Cam was a sheriff's deputy in some smaller town north of here. He got drummed out for some reason or another and lost his way."

"Where'd you hear about this?"

"He's sweet on one of the dancers at the Stamper. She's a friend of mine and goes on about him whenever she gets the opportunity. Come to think of it," she added thoughtfully, "that may be a little biased in his direction. What I know for certain is that Cam brought some money along with him and Bo talked him into staking his operation."

"You mean with the roulette table?"

"That and a few other games in town. The percentages those three haven't bought have been taken at the end of a gun. James's gun."

"He's a killer?" Slocum asked.

She scoffed. "According to some. But that's only what I've heard from the folks around the theater. They're either afraid of him or they're one of his ladies, so you decide how much of it to believe. One thing I know for certain is that James is a bloodthirsty pimp who'd just as soon hit a woman as he would scratch an itch. Hits men just as well, but doesn't enjoy it as much. Daddy says he's shot three in the street outside the theater, but I only witnessed two."

Ticking his points off on his fingers, Slocum said, "So Cam brought the seed money, James brought his own business and a gun, while Bo had the brains to expand their interests into other avenues. Interesting."

"You think so? I think those three bastards mean to take away my family's livelihood!"

Slocum leaned back to get a better look at her. "And just a few moments ago, you were talking about them like they were just another couple of rough men you've been watching."

"That's when I assumed you were just getting ready to take them down a few notches. And besides," Eve added, "I was only watching them so I might be able to help when the time came to do something about Daddy's problem."

Curling an arm around her, Slocum said, "Well you did the right thing. Now is the time to do something, and all that watching you did will be a big help."

"Really?"

"Yes. If there's anything else you can tell me, go right ahead. Every little bit will be an advantage since they know next to nothing about me."

Although she curled against him, Eve was tensing up again. "They might know something about you. Your name will have spread around the theater by now, and it won't take much asking around to hear some other things."

"Rumors and tall tales mostly," Slocum replied. "Trust me. I've heard plenty of them myself, and less than half of them even dipped a toe in the truth. If Bo and those others believe what they hear, it'll still work in my favor. Now, what about the rest of the spying you've done? Got any more stories?"

"Plenty. For one, did you know that when Cam was a deputy for . . . what are you doing?"

As Slocum lay with his body pressed against hers, he could feel Eve's generous curves brushing against him. When she shifted her hips, the motion sparked something in him that brought his erection back to life. "You can keep talking," he said. "I'm listening."

"I don't think you are."

"All right," he said as he rolled her onto her back and climbed on top of her. "You caught me."

Eve smiled widely and spread her legs. "Well then," she purred as his stiff member slid into her, "since you're caught I better put you to work."

4

Eve did have plenty of good information about Bo and his two partners. They'd gotten into the theater through some of the dancing girls who worked for James. A gentleman to a fault, Terrance had trusted one of those girls when she'd batted her eyelashes at him and asked for Bo to be given a chance to run a roulette game at the Stamper. After that, the other two had set up shop and refused to leave. Eve had had more to report, but Slocum missed a good portion of it due to some very interesting distractions.

When he returned to the theater, it was early evening. The show was in full swing and loud enough for him to hear the music from the street. Before wading into all of that commotion, Slocum stood outside and pulled in a few breaths of fresh air. At least, it was fresh by Chicago standards. He choked down as much of it as he could and was about to head inside when he noticed a single steady face in the stream of people passing in front of the theater.

The man stood a few inches above most of the crowd, his height accentuated even more by the domed bowler hat he wore. Although obscured by the crowd, the man's light brown suit appeared to be about two sizes too big for the frame upon which it hung. His face might have been friendly under normal circumstances. When it was pointed at Slocum, however, a subtle scowl crept in to twist his mouth into a tight line.

A warning sounded in the back of Slocum's head. Knowing better than to ignore such things, he turned on his heels and began walking down the street. After he'd passed the theater, Slocum looked over his shoulder as if casually examining one of the other buildings. Sure enough, the young man in the brown suit was following him. Slocum hardly broke his stride as he faced forward and continued walking.

There was just over half a moon glowing in the sky and plenty of stars to give the overhead blackness a glow. It was a cool night with just enough moisture in the air to stick to Slocum's face as he rounded the corner and headed for an even busier part of town. He'd been to Chicago a few times, but wasn't so familiar with the city to know all of its nooks and crannies. He could see enough to know he wasn't headed for the fancy district, since most of the people surrounding him eyed him as if he was the freshest hunk of meat to be set upon the table. They kept their distance for the most part, which actually disappointed Slocum.

Instead of waiting for folks to come to him, Slocum approached one of the larger groups gathered around the front of a saloon. The closer he got to the place, the more odors he could pick out of the air. Burned tobacco and perfume were chief among those smells, but the distinct scent of opium caught his attention. A quick survey of the crowd showed him that most of the men gathered around that saloon weren't wearing hats, so Slocum removed his and stooped slightly so he could blend in with the others. The crowd parted without a fuss and a few shoved Slocum back, but it was only a matter of seconds before he was completely surrounded. As soon as he'd waded most of the way through, Slocum circled back toward the outer edge again.

He waited there for a few seconds. It wasn't difficult since most of the men were trying to get a look inside the saloon at some exotic woman servicing paying customers and doing her best to attract more business from the street. Just as he started to worry that he'd lost the man in the brown suit for good, the fellow rounded a corner and nervously glanced up and down the street.

Pushing back against an anxious drunk, Slocum hid himself just long enough for the other man to pass him by. As soon as the fellow in the suit moved away from the crowd, Slocum stepped out of it, slapped his hat back onto his head, and dropped a heavy hand onto the man's shoulder.

"Looking for someone?" he asked.

The man in the brown suit wheeled around and reflexively grabbed for the holster strapped around his waist.

Slocum defused that little problem with a simple slap that knocked the man's hand away from the .32 hanging at his side. He scolded the man. "No need for that. We haven't even met."

"I know who you are," the man said with a poor attempt to keep his voice from wavering.

"And I think I know you as well," Slocum replied. "At least, I've got a good idea who sent you."

"Nobody sent me."

Draping an arm around the man's shoulders so he could guide him down the street, Slocum said, "You'll have to come up with something better than that."

The man tried to get to his gun, but Slocum was too close for him to make an easy reach for his holster. Since he wasn't quite ready to fight for the pistol just yet, he continued walking alongside Slocum. "I tell you, nobody sent me."

"Does Bo count as nobody?"

"I don't know who that is."

Slocum stopped and pushed the man so his back knocked against the front of a darkened storefront. It could have been an office of some kind, but he wasn't concerned about that.

Rather than look at the building, Slocum studied the other man's face and mannerisms. "You don't know Bo or James? What about Cam?"

"I don't care who those men are. I know who you are, though."

"Do you, now?"

When the man nodded, the brim of his rounded hat tapped against the wall behind him. "You're John Slocum. You've killed innocent men in cold blood and left children without mothers."

"I'm no murderer," Slocum growled, "and I'll have words with whoever's saying otherwise."

The man pulled himself up by the bootstraps and forced a defiant glare onto his face. "You'll answer for what you've done, that's for certain."

"And you'd be the one to see to that?"

The man nodded again.

"Do I get to know the name of the man judging me?" Slocum asked. When the other man froze in his spot, Slocum added, "Or are you ready to walk away after tracking me down this far?"

The flinch that darted across the man's face spoke of an uneasiness that passed as he scooted along the wall to put some distance between himself and Slocum. "There's a price on your head and I aim to collect it. I'm giving you the chance to come along with me now before there's any bloodshed."

"How generous of you."

"I've got men watching you from a couple different rooftops, just like in Fort Griffin."

"And what happened in Fort Griffin?"

"Don't play dumb with me. Eight men died in Fort Griffin by your hand and you'll answer for it. I saw the notices myself."

"You're a bounty hunter?" Slocum asked without trying to hide his disbelief.

The other man nodded, albeit reluctantly.

Slocum glanced up and down the street, but couldn't find any hint of someone backing the man's play. "If you are a bounty hunter, there's no need for you to make up some tall tale about Fort Griffin. I've done plenty more to earn those bounties."

"I know what you did and I'm not the only one." When Slocum shifted his weight, the man in the brown suit twitched anxiously. "You can come with me or the others will hunt you down."

After rubbing his chin, Slocum asked, "What's your name?"

"Michael Harper." Narrowing his eyes, he added, "I bet that name brings you right back to Fort Griffin, doesn't it?"

"Can't say that it does." Slocum placed his hand on the grip of his Colt Navy and stepped back. "I've got other business to tend to. If you want to try and use that gun of yours, do it quick."

For a moment, Slocum thought Harper had run out of steam. His bluff had been called, he'd lost the element of surprise, and he sure didn't seem like much of a bounty hunter. All of those things didn't give a whole lot for the fellow in the rumpled brown suit to hang onto. Even so, he eased into a sideways stance and nodded once as if quietly making a pact with himself.

"Damn it," Slocum grunted as he lunged forward to snap a fist into Harper's face. The punch landed with a sharp cracking sound and was quickly followed by the dull thump of Harper's back against the wall. Even as he blinked and tried to speak, it was plain to see that he was out on his feet. After a few more seconds, he didn't even have his feet to support him.

Harper slid down the wall to form a heap at its base. As Slocum collected the .32 from the supposed bounty hunter's holster, he looked around to see if he'd drawn any interest from other nearby locals. The women inside the opium den must have been working awfully hard, because most of the men in the vicinity were still looking inside that place. Then again, the folks in Chicago could have just been accustomed to the sight of one man knocking the other into unconsciousness.

Slocum was about to tuck the .32 under his belt, but thought differently of it. As he hurried toward the Stamper Theater, he checked to make sure the gun was loaded and ready to be fired. Instead of tucking it somewhere it could be so easily found, Slocum reached around to slip it under his belt at the small of his back. The pistol was smaller than his Colt Navy and settled into its spot fairly well.

The more Slocum thought about what Michael had said, the less sense it made. Sure, he'd been to Fort Griffin, but he didn't know what eight men the bounty hunter was talking about. It nagged at him so much that he slowed his pace so he could have a few more seconds in which to think back to nearly every visit to Texas. There simply wasn't enough time for Slocum to sift through all of that and still get to the Stamper for Bo's next shift behind his wheel. According to Terrance, Bo's habits were damn near set in stone. Unless Bo wanted to admit defeat already, he'd be sure to show up at his normal time as if nothing had happened.

Just to be on the safe side, Slocum stretched his neck to look around him in every direction. He looked up and down the street, across to the other side of the street, down to the near and far corners, even up along the rooftops. The only thing that did for him was put a mighty painful kink in his neck. The rest of Chicago seemed content to go about its own business without disturbing him in the least.

By the time he arrived at the Stamper, Slocum was glad to hear raucous music rolling out of the place like a wall of smoke. A group of women were singing loud enough to strain their voices just to be heard above the sorry excuse for an orchestra, and the audience was showing their appreciation with even louder cries. Slocum walked in through the front door and was immediately set upon.

"Where have you been?" Terrance asked as he stepped up and placed himself between Slocum and the rest of the theater.

"In my hotel room. You don't pay me enough to stand here without kicking my feet up every now and then."

"I'm also not paying you to consort with my daughter!"

"What was that?"

Even though he could hear Terrance well enough over the noise, Slocum cupped a hand to his ear and grimaced when the other man repeated himself. "Sorry," Slocum said, "but I think that whiskey is hitting me harder than usual."

Terrance eyed Slocum suspiciously, but didn't press the issue. Slocum considered himself lucky that Eve had made herself scarce at that moment, so the subject could remain dropped for a while.

"I see the roulette wheel is being spun again," he pointed out.

There was no need for any other distractions. The problem that had brought Slocum to Chicago was big enough to command all of the other man's attention. "That's Cam back there now, but Bo and James are lurking about somewhere. They've been asking folks about you."

"I figured they might. What about their other friends?"

"Other friends?"

"Surely there's got to be some other partners with them three. Stupidity loves company."

Chuckling at Slocum's twist on a common phrase, Terrance said, "They don't pull in enough money to keep more'n three interested at a time."

"What about the women James runs through here?"

Judging by the look on Terrance's face, those girls weren't exactly welcome additions to his payroll. "That's the only way I'm coming out ahead in this deal. The girls slip me a percentage of what they make in exchange for their room and board."

"Just room and board?"

"Plus the occasional helping hand from the boys who protect the theater's gambling interests."

Craning his neck to get a complete look at the busy room, Slocum asked, "And where might these strapping young men be?"

"Standing at their posts, ready to take a swing at anyone other than the three that deserve it the most. It's been that way ever since James damn near killed one of them."

"Sounds like a sloppy arrangement," Slocum grumbled.

"Why do you think I went through the trouble of finding you? Once those three are tossed out of here for good, things will get back to running the way they're supposed to be run. You make it a good enough show to discourage anyone else looking to horn in on my theater and I'll be much obliged."

"That'll cost extra. Ever heard of a man named Mike Harper?"

After a confused scowl, Terrance asked, "Who?"

"Didn't think so."

"What have we here?" Bo hollered from one of the card tables near the edge of the room. It wasn't until he shoved his chair back and got to his feet that the skinny wheel spinner set himself apart from the other card players. The wide brim on Bo's hat went a long way in keeping his face hidden, and when he removed it, he flashed a toothy smile. Slocum doubted his sudden bout of courage was merely fortunate timing.

Sure enough, Slocum picked out James stomping down the stairs while hitching his suspenders up over his shoulders.

"Thought you were smart enough to stay away, John Slocum," Bo said while stepping away from his table. He was still careful to keep it between him and the man in his sights, though. "I know that's your name, Slocum. I know plenty about you."

While walking toward the card table, Slocum wasn't able to keep his eye on the stairs that emptied to a platform on the bar's side of the room. He was, however, able to position himself so he could see any movement from that side of the room on the edge of his field of vision. Once he was close enough to speak instead of shout at Bo, Slocum said, "You found out my name. I get that much. How about I have a quick word with you?"

"Now you wanna talk, huh? Before you were quicker to draw your pistol."

Banking on whatever Bo might have heard about him, Slocum put a steely edge to his voice and said, "I could do that if you like. It'd make for a quicker end to the evening for one of us."

Bo wanted to keep his scowl in place, but James wasn't close enough to make him so comfortable. The gunman was still picking his way through the people gathered near the stage, who didn't seem to have any clue about or interest in what was happening in the rest of the theater. Rather than destroy the bravado he'd worked so hard to build, Bo nodded and walked with Slocum toward the front door. He stopped short of stepping outside, taking up a position with his back to the wall beside the door. "What is it you want to say?"

"I found the man you sent to follow me."

After a flicker of a twitch, Bo replied, "I don't know what you're talking about."

"Michael Harper. We had a nice little talk."

The flicker came again, which was more than enough to convince Slocum of Bo's ignorance on the matter. Steering things back on course, he said, "Never mind that. I've got a proposition for you."

Grateful for talk he could understand, Bo replied, "If you

want to become one of my partners, I think you may need to talk to someone else before me."

Slocum had no trouble spotting James struggling to cross the room. Not only was the theater most crowded in the area near the stage, but James was obviously too drunk to walk straight. The anger flared like a red beacon on his cheeks, and whenever someone stepped in front of him or nudged him when he tried to pass by, James would stop to give them a piece of his mind.

All of that only bought Slocum the time he needed. "No, someone told me you're the man with the business sense," he said.

Bo couldn't help but puff his chest out with pride.

Leaning forward and dropping his voice, as if bringing Bo in on a precious secret, Slocum told him, "I've been paid to get you out of this theater and I will most definitely get the job done. All you need to do is find somewhere else to spin your wheel, leave this place alone, and I'll split my fee with you. Your men will get your hooks into another place and we'll all be a little richer."

"How much richer?"

"Half of my fee is a hundred and fifty dollars," Slocum said with such certainty that he probably could have gotten the lie to float in front of a judge and jury. "That's fifty for each of you."

"Fifty? That's it?"

"Fine. You'll get two hundred and your partners will get fifty. Just make sure they don't find out," Slocum added with a nudge.

James was getting close enough for his voice to consistently break through the noise passing for music in the place. Glancing back in that direction, Bo dropped his tone to a fierce whisper when he said, "We're making a hell of a lot more than that now."

"A bit of money in a living man's hand is worth a lot

more than a bigger amount stuffed into a dead one's pockets. This is an easy payday for both of us. All I need is to look like I'm holding my end up to get some bigger jobs later on. You pick up and move somewhere else and live to see another day. Maybe I'll owe you a favor."

Now, that registered with Bo like it would in the mind of any businessman. Favors could be more valuable than gold if they were owed by the right people. And since Bo seemed like one of the men who believed the rumors he'd heard about John Slocum, he had to be thinking he was looking at a very valuable favor indeed. When James's voice exploded nearby like a stick of dynamite, Bo matched it with some bellowing of his own. "You're damn right you'll owe me! And I aim to collect." In a hasty whisper, he added, "There's an opium den not far from here. You know the one?"

"Yeah," Slocum replied. "I do."

"Meet me there this time tomorrow and we'll make our arrangements. Bring the money."

"What's that about money?" James snarled. His breaths were coming to him in haggard gulps. Struggling through the uncooperative crowd had left him looking like a disheveled wild man. Setting his sights on Slocum, James plastered a smile onto his face and said, "I didn't think you'd have the sand to show your face around here again."

Ignoring the bait being dangled in front of him, Slocum said, "Really? Guess I'll leave then."

Under any other circumstances, Slocum would have rather died than give in to the likes of James so quickly. This time, however, it was worth it just to see the befuddled expression on the pimp's sweaty face.

5

Slocum didn't stay away from the Stamper Theater for long. He walked outside and went down the street just far enough to let him know if he was being followed. After all that had happened so far, his senses were keen enough to pick up on the movement of every drunk in the shadows and the sound of every hacking wheeze from behind closed doors. If someone was following him, they were better than the sort of killer who would work with Bo or his partners.

Satisfied that he was on his own, Slocum circled around the block and approached the Stamper from another angle. He didn't go in through the front door, but knocked on one of the back entrances instead. After a few sharp raps of his knuckles, the door opened just wide enough for a cautious eye to peer out at him. The crack widened so Slocum could also see a sliver of smooth skin, and painted lips that parted to ask, "Is that you, Mr. Slocum?"

"Yes and call me John."

The young woman who opened the door did so quickly and stepped aside while lowering her eyes. "Eve said you were in town. She also said . . . well . . ."

"I can just imagine what she said," Slocum replied while stepping inside.

"Did you get locked out or something?"

"Isn't it early for Terrance to lock up?"

"Yes, but that would explain why you didn't come in through the front."

The door opened into a cramped backstage area filled mostly with dressing rooms for the dancing girls and a few small storage closets. Some of the narrow doors along the tight hallway looked like they might open into offices, but Slocum wasn't about to check behind each one. He simply let his ears lead him to the source of the loudest noise and his eyes draw him to the light pouring in from the larger room on the other side of the velvet curtain. "Had to sneak around back," he told the young lady.

She was more than a foot shorter than him and had wispy brown hair and finely rounded cheekbones. Her skin was smooth and pale, due to the powder she wore on some very appealing natural traits. Thin, dark red lips curled into a cute little smile as she whispered, "If you're trying to hide from Eve, you should be safe back here."

"She's got that kind of reputation, huh?"

"It's obvious she's sunk her teeth into you."

"More than once," Slocum replied with a wink. "But no, I'm not hiding from Eve. I'd appreciate it if you didn't let anyone know I was here, though."

She nodded quickly. "I can do that, sure."

"Where's a good spot for me to look in on the gamblers?"

"Which ones?"

"The roulette players."

Her eyes grew wide, and when she pulled in a breath, the young lady quickly covered her mouth with her hand. "Is this about Bo and Cam?"

"Yep. Are they still here?"

Without saying a word, she pointed straight up.

"They're upstairs?" Slocum asked.

She nodded.

He reflexively lowered his voice to match the young woman's. "Can they hear us from up there?"

Leaning in close to him, she whispered, "Probably, since we can hear plenty that goes on upstairs. Banging, giggling, hollering."

"What about talking?"

"Sometimes."

Slocum looked at the ceiling over his head, as if he could see straight through to the rooms above. "Would you happen to know where Bo and those other two might go to talk without folks listening in?"

"Maybe. Why?"

"Because I want to listen in."

When she saw the mischievous grin on his face, the young woman quickly grew one of her own. "We can try this way," she told him as she led Slocum down the hall and toward one of the narrow doors that he'd spotted coming in. They were in one of the corners at the back of the building. On stage, the song shifted into a rowdier number and the audience showed their appreciation in all sorts of boisterous ways. Those added layers of noise gave the woman some courage as she pulled one of the doors open and motioned for Slocum to follow. Sure enough, it was a storage space, just as he'd figured.

She went into the large closet, pushing aside a bunch of brooms and mops that had been resting against the wall in a clump. Slocum got inside with her and eased the door shut so only a bit of light from the hallway trickled inside. That served to filter out some of the noise from the stage show, but also made her shift uncomfortably from one foot to the other.

"It's all right," he assured her. When he stroked her arm

to settle her nerves, he felt her rub against his hand rather than pull away from it. Apparently, she wasn't uncomfortable for the reasons he'd thought.

Footsteps knocked against the floor above them and were much too heavy to have been made by a woman. Others shifted overhead as well, soon to be followed by deep, muffled voices.

"Lots of rooms were built one on top of the other in this place," she whispered. "James uses one for himself and it's right above us."

The steps shuffled a bit, but the voices stopped. Then more steps knocked against the floor, and were soon followed by the creak of a door. Now that he was paying such close attention to the sounds on the second floor, Slocum wondered if they were always so easy to hear, in every place. It made him think back to all the noise he'd made in hotel rooms, with plenty of folks going about their business directly beneath his bed.

Although that thought brought to mind plenty of peculiar notions, Slocum didn't allow them to distract him as he listened to what was going on. The young woman in there with him squirmed, and every rustle of her clothes and every movement of her body was a distraction. Slocum took hold of her in both hands just to keep her still. When she tried to speak, he silenced her by placing a finger on her lips. Judging by the way she stood and looked up at him, she wasn't entirely opposed to their time in the dark.

"What's your name?" he whispered.

"Maddie."

"I need you to be quiet, all right, Maddie?"

"All . . ." Rather than say another word, she nodded and leaned a little closer to him.

Slocum couldn't make out exactly what the voices above him were saying. Every now and then, he thought he could make out a word, but he never caught enough to put together a whole sentence. The parts he did catch were barely

enough to tell him Bo and the other two were the ones doing the talking. For that, he had to rely on what Maddie told
him. There wasn't an obvious reason for her to lie and
Slocum doubted that there were lots of groups of three men
spending time in a room together when there were so many
women to be had. Also, the voices weren't rowdy or wavering enough to be coming from three drunks. That knocked
another healthy portion of the theater's customers from con-
sideration.

What Slocum could hear was the tone of those voices,
which came in clipped chunks as steps paced toward the
back of the room above. It didn't take much imagination for
Slocum to imagine that the men had tossed out a few curt
greetings, started their discussion, and were now making
their way to preferred spots or chairs. A few throats were
cleared and the conversation continued.

Slocum found himself looking toward the ceiling, but all
that did was agitate the kink in his neck. He lowered his
head, cocked it so one ear was aimed upward, and closed
his eyes. Maddie let out a little sigh and put one hand on
Slocum's elbow. He took a quick peek to see what she was
doing, but didn't get anything besides a nervous smile from
the young lady.

One voice droned on for a few seconds like the sound of
a distant waterwheel. Slocum was certain that was Bo,
whispering in a hiss just as he'd done when conspiring with
Slocum earlier. After that, a gruffer voice rolled completely
over the first. That would be James. Not only was the large
man impatient, but he accented it by stomping back and
forth across the floor. Bo's voice rose to try and be heard
over James, until they were both loud enough to make Slocum completely certain that he was listening to the right
group.

It was also clear to him that the men were not engaged
in a friendly conversation. Bo kept a strong, steady tone
while James exploded in short, angry bursts. Some of those

bursts were loud enough for Slocum to hear every last pro-
fanity. Even Maddie winced at some of the more creative
obscenities.

"Do they argue like this a lot?" Slocum whispered.

"Sometimes, but not this bad. At least, not what I've ever
heard. I can go ask some of the others if—"

"No, no," Slocum said while taking hold of her once
again. "Just stay put."

Although Maddie continued to glance toward the door,
she clearly wasn't in a hurry to dash through it. Instead, she
touched him as if she was reaching for forbidden fruit. It
was well within reason that Eve would have spoken of her
encounters with Slocum to the other girls at the theater.
Since Terrance hadn't come at him with a shotgun yet, Slocum figured all of the women were keeping their mouths
shut around the boss. Keeping a secret from the man in
charge would only make it that much juicier.

The closet became quiet enough for Slocum to make out
more and clearer pieces of the conversation upstairs. Bo's
voice was steady and insistent. Whenever James tried to cut
in, he was silenced by another voice that spoke in clipped,
muffled tones. That had to be Cam. Slocum could easily
picture the former deputy stepping in to keep the peace, but
being rebuffed by the bigger gunman.

Bo finished his piece in a hurry. Every now and then,
Slocum heard his name mentioned along with several refer-
ences to money. Since the news went over about as well as
he would have expected, Slocum guessed the deal was being delivered as he'd intended. James wasn't happy about it
whatsoever, which further told him that the skewed offer
was being made to leave Bo the chief beneficiary and the
other two coming away with a minor profit at best. Slocum
grinned and looked down to Maddie as the footsteps overhead began to disperse.

"I think I heard all I need," he said.

Even after he stepped aside, Maddie remained where she was. "I've heard some things about you," she whispered.

"I figured you might have."

"Eve does a lot of bragging, but I didn't hear anything about you being her property."

"I should damn well hope not."

"I'm guessing you don't want Bo or them other two to know about us listening in on them?"

Glaring at her hard enough for it to be felt in the dark, Slocum asked, "Are you making a threat?"

"Sort of, but I'm not asking much in return."

Then Slocum felt something else in the dark. A small, warm hand slipped between his legs to cup him and massage gently. Her face brightened as she gazed up at him and said, "I see some of Eve's stories were true. All I want is to find out about the rest."

"And that'll keep you quiet to Bo or anyone else about this?"

She nodded, stroking him slowly until his erection strained against the front of his jeans.

Slocum gathered her skirts until he could reach beneath them and start tugging at her undergarments. There was a lot of material to get through, but Maddie was more than happy to help him in his task. By the time his hand finally touched the warm skin between her thighs, she was breathing in quick anticipation. She tried to form words even as her hands fumbled with Slocum's belt and the front of his pants.

"You're . . . This is . . . Oh my . . ." She sighed.

Reaching around to cup her buttocks beneath her skirts, Slocum moved her so Maddie was against a wall. When he lifted her up, she hopped so one leg was propped against an old chair and the other was wrapped around his waist. Her arms encircled the back of his neck and tightened as he plunged every inch of his cock into her. Maddie gasped and held on tight as Slocum thrust between her legs.

There were still a few footsteps overhead and more coming from the hallway just outside the closet door, but Slocum didn't pay them any mind. The upstairs footsteps only meant Bo and the others were still preoccupied, and the ones outside, going back and forth in a stampede, were one group of dancing girls switching out for another. Maddie's face pressed against Slocum's neck as she let out a muffled little groan that barely made enough noise to be heard over everything else.

When Slocum tightened his grip on her, Maddie tightened hers upon him. She may have started off surprised by his sudden move to take her, but Maddie was settling into the situation just fine. Her hips ground in time with his, and she even got him to speed up by pressing her foot against his back in a quickening pace. Soon, her fingers curled against his back and shoulder, to dig her nails into his flesh.

The men upstairs filed out of the room. Just when Slocum thought they were all gone, a few sets of feet shuffled near what was either the doorway or the front of that space. A low, gruff voice spoke to a hesitant one. Apparently, James wanted a word with Cam before stepping out. Slocum couldn't hear any specifics, but James's growling voice reeked of suspicion. After a few seconds, both sets of boots clomped away and the door above Slocum's head slammed shut.

"Good Lord," Maddie sighed into his ear.

As much as he wanted to get a look out at the staircase to see if the other three men were coming back down to the main floor, Slocum didn't leave Maddie prematurely. In fact, she'd gotten into a nice little rhythm of her own and was making him glad he'd decided to spend some extra time in the dark with her. The curves of her backside filled his hands and her muscles strained with an impending orgasm. He held her up just a bit higher against the wall so the rigid shaft of his cock hit her in just the right spot. This wasn't Slocum's first time against a wall, and he knew a trick or two about how to make the experience a memorable one. That trick didn't go unappreciated.

Maddie's arms locked around him firmly enough to make Slocum gulp for air. She pressed herself against him as hard as she could as he pumped into her one more time. When he was all the way in, Slocum stayed there until every inch of her was trembling. As soon as the climax passed, he started to slowly ease out. The warm dampness between her legs glided along his length, teasing him to the end of his own trail. A few more powerful thrusts put him over the edge and nearly got Maddie to spoil their hiding spot with a deep-throated scream. She pressed her mouth against Slocum's shoulder as the next song started on stage.

A minute or two later, Maddie emerged from the closet. She tugged at her skirts and fretted with her hair while glancing up and down the narrow hallway. After a straggling dancing girl rushed past her, she opened the closet door and gave Slocum a few quick waves. "Come on out," she whispered.

Slocum was still buckling his belt as he stepped into what felt like a blazing light. His eyes quickly adjusted to the glare of the lanterns hanging from the walls, which, compared to the inside of the cramped closet, seemed close to high noon. "Not a word of this to anyone, you hear?"

"I won't tell about the listening, but the rest . . ."

Not too concerned about the rest, Slocum patted her on the backside as he walked down the hall and crossed completely behind the stage. As he'd figured, the hallway wrapped around the back of the theater to a small door on the side of the room with the gambling tables. Not only could he see Bo winding his way back to his roulette table, but Slocum also caught sight of James and Cam stomping from the bottom of the staircase toward the bar. Neither of those two was very happy.

"All right then," Slocum said to himself. "Let's see just how deep your loyalties lie."

6

Slocum spent the time leading up to his prearranged meeting carefully. After making a private request of Terrance, he visited a few men in Chicago who might possibly know about someone like Michael Harper. None of them did.

His appointment with Bo was drawing close when Slocum returned to the theater. He strode in through the front doors and found Cam spinning the roulette wheel. James and Bo were nowhere to be found, but he didn't let that concern him. Slocum stepped up to the bar, slapped the polished surface, and was soon greeted by two familiar faces.

The bartender nodded once, but didn't get to do much else before the second man cut him short.

"What are you doing here?" Terrance asked.

"I was about to enjoy some free whiskey."

"That trash is still standing behind my gambling table," the older man said while swinging an arm toward the opposite side of the room.

"Not for much longer."

"So you really intend on meeting Bo later tonight?"

"What makes you think that?"

"I've got my sources."

Slocum looked toward the stage but didn't see Maddie among the girls dancing there. Even so, he doubted she'd found out that much. Since there were plenty of other sources for stray gossip and loose talk, Slocum placed his hands on the bar and waited for his drink. "It won't work out too well if you flap your gums about it, but yeah, I mean to have a word with them in a bit."

Nodding at the bartender, Terrance said, "Give him his whiskey. I'll have one too. So what's this talk gonna be about, John?"

"I plan on taking over this theater with those three idiots. What the hell do you think it'll be about?"

"What I meant is, will this all be over by tomorrow?"

"The sooner the better," Slocum said.

"If so, I've got your money. There'll even be some extra if you could make certain that . . . shall I say . . . any or all of those men aren't able to bother me in the future."

The whiskey was set in front of him, and Slocum lifted it so he could look through the dark liquid at the candle burning on the shelf behind the bartender's head. "You should stick to the theater business and leave assassinations to the professionals."

"It's a simple contract."

"You run a fancy saloon," Slocum told him. "You trying to arrange a murder is anything but simple. Do yourself a favor and spare yourself the pain of getting into a mess like that."

Terrance could tell there was no arguing with him, so he simply nodded and took his drink.

"Did you tell James what I asked you to?" Slocum asked.

"Yes. He's going to be keeping an eye out for Bo after the nine o'clock show."

"Good. I suppose I should be on my way then."

"Should I brace for the worst?"

Slocum looked about at the men Terrance had hired to protect his place. They may have been armed, but if they'd known how to use those guns as anything but stage dressing, the Stamper wouldn't have been in its current predicament. "Things may get worse before they get better. Have them watch the street for the rest of the night."

"And after that?"

"You'll know well enough once it gets that far."

With that, Slocum set down his glass and left the theater. He didn't have to look to know he was being watched by Terrance, Cam, and undoubtedly several other sets of eyes. The walk to the opium den felt twice as long as it actually was. Every step of the way, Slocum was ready to be ambushed, shot at, or any number of things that could very possibly ruin his night. None of those events came to pass, however, before the familiar scent of acrid smoke caught his nose. The crowd outside the opium den was smaller than before, which meant Bo didn't have anywhere to hide.

"So," Slocum said as he approached the skinny man, "did you have a chance to talk things over with your partners?"

"Yeah. They weren't happy, but they agreed. Where's the money?"

Digging into his pocket, Slocum stretched out a portion of his advance so Bo and several of the glassy-eyed customers could see it. The roulette spinner snatched the money away and tucked it under the flap of his vest.

"How quick before you'll pack up your wheel?"

"Don't worry about that," Bo replied. "I'll hold my end up."

As the skinny man hurried away, Slocum said, "Be sure that you do. There's plenty of work for men who can be trusted." He wasn't certain what effect those words had on the other man, but every little bit of uncertainty he could sow at this point was a good investment.

Slocum watched the other man go as if Bo was a toy he'd wound up and sent on its way. After Bo rounded a corner, Slocum set out after him. Bo didn't try to mask his route and led Slocum right back to the Stamper Theater to find James standing on the boardwalk waiting for him.

"Where've you been?" James asked.

"I need to have a word with you," Bo replied. "Meet me inside."

"I got a few words for you, too."

"Inside!"

"No," James said as he planted his feet and placed his hand on the grip of his holstered pistol. "Right here. Right now."

The streets were never clear, but there weren't many folks out and about at this time of night. A few horses ambled along one side of the street and small groups of people walked past the Stamper Theater without taking much notice of the men in front of it.

"What's gotten into you?" Bo demanded.

James was quick to shoot back with "What's gotten into your pockets?"

This was right about the time that Slocum rounded the corner and got close enough to the theater to hear what was being said. Rather than interfere, he picked a spot across the street and settled in to watch the show.

"I heard you aim to hold out on me." When the front door opened so the youngest member of the trio could step outside, James added, "Me and Cam, that is."

"Who told you that?" Bo asked.

"Terrance."

"Why the hell would you believe him?"

"He says he had Slocum pay to get us out of here and that your cut was triple what you told me and Cam it was. Empty your pockets and prove me wrong."

"How do you know I've got anything?" Bo asked.

"That's what I heard. The old man that runs this theater may not be reliable, but I don't have any trouble believing you'd double-cross us where money's concerned."

"You don't, huh?"

James stepped toward Bo to stand with his shoulders squared and his hand ready to skin the gun at his hip. Without taking his eyes away from Bo, he said, "Cam, have a look at what's in his pockets."

Slocum smiled at the simplicity of his plan as well as how simply it had been put into action. Then again, manipulating minds as simple as James's and Bo's wasn't much of a test. The intent had been to place a wedge between the members of the gang by setting one of them against the others in any possible way. Once someone as rowdy as James found out about Bo's trespass, the wedge would be driven in nice and deep. To be honest, Slocum had expected to need a few more go-rounds before the gang was ready to nip at its own heels. By the looks of it, though, he only needed to wait for all that money to be found for the show to start. He'd slipped even more money into the bundle than he'd told Bo about, so that should really get things going.

Cam walked over to Bo, said a few things that were too soft for Slocum to hear, and started digging in the skinny man's pockets.

"John Slocum!"

The voice had come from down the street in the opposite direction from the opium den. Slocum looked over there to find a lean man striding toward him. It was Michael Harper.

Slocum's eyes darted back and forth between Harper and Bo. Even though James was watching carefully from the front of the Stamper, his two partners were preoccupied with what they were doing. If Harper continued to draw attention, however, that wouldn't last long.

Slocum shook his head, pulled his hat down a bit more over his eyes, and stepped back. Some people were walking by and would pass in front of him before too long. If he could keep quiet for just a bit longer, he might be able to mosey along with them so as not to interrupt Bo and James's impending squabble.

"I found you once," Harper said. "I found you this time, and I can find you again. Will I have to keep chasing you around like a scalded dog?"

Any desire to walk away or try to hide dried up from Slocum's chest quicker than a splash of water on the desert floor. He stood up tall, walked up to Harper, and snarled, "You were lucky to get away once, boy. Why the hell would you want to tempt fate again?"

James shifted his attention to what was happening across the street. "Slocum? What're you doing lurking in the shadows?"

Bo looked back and forth so quickly that he damn near snapped his own neck. "Were you setting me up?"

"Aww shit," Slocum growled under his breath.

The only way for things to go to hell quicker after that would have been if the devil had clawed his way up from the pit to drag them there personally. James drew his pistol and fired a shot before he'd even given himself a chance to fix his eyes on a target. The shot didn't draw any blood, but it did a real good job of stirring things up. Cam and Bo put their potential differences aside so they could skin their own weapons. When Harper reached for the pistol holstered under his arm, Slocum didn't have any choice other than to jump into the battle feet-first.

Although he could have drawn his Colt Navy with more than enough speed to do some damage, Slocum took the opportunity to disarm one of his opponents in a more direct fashion. He rushed at Harper, grabbed the bounty hunter's arm, and pulled it so the .22 he'd drawn was pointed toward the upper windows of the theater. From there, he twisted Harper's wrist and followed up with a sharp kick to his knee. The gun slipped from his hand before he collapsed under his own weight.

Slocum caught Harper's weapon before it hit the ground; then he drew his Colt and rushed along the boardwalk to avoid shooting a group of men who'd been staggering down the street. The instant he had a clear shot, he aimed the Colt Navy and fired. The pistol bucked against his palm, spitting a round through the air that came within an inch of creasing Bo's scalp. It got close enough to send the skinny man straight down where he scrambled for cover. Cam dashed in another direction, but James walked straight ahead.

"You wanna do this now, Slocum?" James hollered as if enjoying the sound of his own voice. "I'll put you straight out of your misery!" He fired without pause or any concern as to where his bullets landed. One of them came within a few feet of the post that Slocum leaned against for protection, but the rest only shattered glass in nearby windows or knocked holes into walls.

Slocum fired the gun in his left hand without expecting to hit anything. He pulled that trigger just to make enough noise to scatter the locals before one or more of them caught a bullet. His efforts proved to be very effective, sending drunks and working girls alike racing away from the Stamper Theater. When Harper's .22 ran dry, Slocum threw it away and shifted to the Colt in his right hand. Instead of firing that one as quickly as possible, he lined up his shot and squeezed his trigger carefully. James caught the bullet high enough in his left arm for it to create a messy wound as it ripped straight through and came out the other side. The pimp was spun around by the impact and fell to one knee.

Bo was yelling something across the street, but Slocum couldn't hear him over the wailing of panicked folks in the street and the shouting of a few men who tried to pull the reins back on the chaos. Slocum assumed those men were authorities of some sort, but he didn't intend on sticking around long enough to get involved with them any more than that. When it became clear nobody was listening to him, Bo set his sights on Slocum and started firing.

More than anything, Slocum had wanted to set his simple plan into motion and leave Chicago richer than when he'd arrived. Not only did it seem he was going to fail in the task given to him by Terrance, but Slocum was also worried about leaving Chicago without being carried away in a pine box. The remaining two gunmen didn't concern Slocum as much as they'd inconvenienced him. Shooting them would have been easier, and he could have done it a while ago. But getting them to tear each other down would have made less of a mess and kept Terrance out of any entanglements with the law. Now, thanks to some loud, ill-timed words, he didn't have a say in the matter.

And just when he thought he'd gotten a firm grip on the situation again, Slocum was thrown off his game. From behind some crates stacked in front of the building next to the Stamper, Cam fired a couple shots at Slocum that chipped at the post in front of him. He responded to that by leaning out of his cover and using the Colt Navy to punch a few holes through those crates. Cam fired his last shot at the same time James picked himself up from being sent to the ground. No sooner had the pimp lifted his gun hand than Terrance exploded through the front door of the theater.

"That's enough!" the older man shouted.

"Get back inside," Bo said.

Terrance responded to that with a fiery shotgun blast. Slocum reflexively dropped when he heard the noise, but he was still scraped by several stray pieces of lead. One of the windows behind him shattered, but none of that compared to the hell that had been visited upon Bo.

Standing closest to Terrance, the skinny wheel spinner caught the brunt of the blast. He was knocked off his feet, sent several yards into the street, and hit the dirt in a bloody pile. The sight of him was gruesome enough to stop everything else in the vicinity. Men who'd been scrambling for cover or fighting to get away couldn't help but gawk at Bo's twitching remains. Even Slocum leaned away from his post with his arm stretched in front of him as if he'd forgotten what it was he'd been aiming at. To make the sight even more captivating, bits of the money that Slocum had given Bo fluttered through the air like so many dead leaves before sticking to the wet mud in the nearby ditches.

Cam had only been a few long strides away from where Bo was standing. Now he stumbled toward his fallen partner, gripping his pistol with just enough strength to keep it from falling through his fingers. He stared down at Bo's body and would have taken a shot at Slocum if not for the metallic click of Terrance's second shotgun hammer being pulled back.

"You men won't step foot in my place again," Terrance warned. "All these people here saw you shooting this street up. What I did was in self-defense."

"That's right," one of the people near the Stamper said. "I'll be a witness."

"Me too," one of Terrance's girls chimed in. "They were going to kill someone."

"Sure was!"

"I'll get the law myself and tell 'em what happened!"

So many people were talking that Slocum couldn't keep track of them all. He had other things to worry about; namely, the dandy bounty hunter who struggled to regain his footing. Before Harper could get his wits about him, Slocum stomped over and hauled him to his feet. "Couldn't leave well enough alone, huh? You had to start this whole mess by coming after me!"

"You're the one who started the mess," Harper replied. "You killed those men in Fort Griffin."

"I don't know what the hell you're talking about!"

"You're a coward and a liar!" the bounty hunter spat.

Even as the street filled with people and James started swinging at whoever got close enough to try and disarm him, Slocum grabbed two handfuls of Harper's shirt and held him up so he could continue his conversation uninterrupted. "I won't abide that kind of talk from any bounty hunter! Men like you will say any damn thing just so long as you can get your money! You'll kill and steal and lie more than most of the men you track down. The only thing separating you from them is some goddamn piece of paper with a notice on it. Come to think of it, where's the notice declaring the reward for me?"

A shot was fired from farther down the street, but Slocum hardly flinched. James and Cam fled down the street, shouting for everyone to stay out of their way and firing wildly to back up their demand. By now, Terrance was being backed up by all of his own men. The theater's guards were more than ready to wave their guns around when the real threat seemed content to scamper in the opposite direction.

"Where's the notice?" Slocum snarled as he shook Harper like a rag doll.

"You know what you did."

"I wanna know where you're getting your ideas. If you're some kind of bounty hunter, you can't just go after any man you please. What the hell made you come after me? I wanna know!"

When Harper started to reach for his jacket pocket, Slocum knocked away his hand and dug into the pocket himself. He found the folded sheet of paper right away, pulled it out of Harper's jacket, and shook it out until he could read what had been printed on its wrinkled surface. Instead of a proper reward notice, it was a hastily drawn sketch of several men standing in a smoke-filled street. Most of those men were lying on their backs or on their sides with blood pooling around them. One of the only figures on their feet held a smoking gun in each hand and was twice as large as any of the rest. The words above the crude picture were "*Six-Gun Devil*: Eight men killed in Fort Griffin showdown."

"This isn't a reward notice!" Slocum said. No matter what else was going on around him, he wasn't about to take his eyes off of Harper. No amount of shouting, cursing, running, or other commotion was going to distract him now that he was this close to the bounty hunter who'd turned his entire Chicago visit into a farce.

What angered Slocum even more was the fact that Harper didn't appear to realize what he'd done. He merely nodded and found a way to look down his nose at Slocum despite the fact that he was the one dangling from another man's fist. "It's all in the print. If you can't read it, that's not my concern."

Tightening his grip on Harper to the point where he was close to tearing the man in half, Slocum growled, "I can read, damn you. If it takes me too long to find what I'm after, I might as well choke the life out of you and read through every last word at my leisure."

"Under the picture," Harper quickly said. "Second line."

Slocum found the second line of typewritten print beneath the picture and read it. "This says I've got prices on my head from half the states in the Union. What the hell is that supposed to mean?"

"It means you've caused enough trouble to make the man rich who puts an end to you."

After stuffing the notice into his pocket, Slocum got a better grip on Harper's shirt and slammed him against the closest wall. "How many times do I gotta tell you I didn't do whatever it is you think happened in Fort Griffin?"

Harper's smug grin and slow shake of his head was almost enough to make Slocum put a bullet through him. "That's what all the outlaws say," he sneered.

"Then I guess I might as well have the same fun as those killers would have at your expense." With that, he brought his Colt Navy up to Harper's chin and glared directly into his eyes.

Then, a hand settled on his shoulder, and Terrance's calm voice cut through the rest of the commotion filling the street. "It's all over, John. He's not one of the men we were after."

"I know, but—"

"Then let him go," Terrance insisted. "There's been enough excitement for one night."

Slocum let out a breath and felt his blind rage settle into the pit of his stomach. It was still there, but not close enough to the surface to dictate his actions. He let go of Harper.

"Where's my gun?" Harper asked.

Amazed at the other man's gall, Slocum replied through gritted teeth, "Tossed it into the street."

"Not that one. The .32 you took from me."

Slocum reached behind his back to pull the .32 out from where it was nestled at the base of his spine. Tossing it to him, Slocum prayed for Harper to make a move that was wrong enough to justify him putting a bullet through the dandy's face. When the bounty hunter started to walk away, Slocum pointed to Terrance and said, "This man saved your damn life. Better give him proper respect."

Even though Harper tipped his bowler hat at the theater owner after collecting his .32, Slocum still wanted to knock the man's head off.

7

Late the next afternoon, Slocum stood at the spot against the bar he'd staked out for his own. With the deathly glare affixed on his face as he stood in his spot and drank, there wasn't anyone else in the Stamper willing to challenge him. He kept one elbow propped against the bar and his eyes pointed toward the front window. Nobody walking up or down Halstead escaped his notice. Likewise, anyone setting foot on Twelfth Street couldn't cast a wayward glance at the Stamper without Slocum knowing about it.

Terrance ambled over to the bar and stood for several seconds without making a sound. Finally, he cleared his throat and began drumming his fingers on the polished wooden surface.

"Before you start whistling a tune," Slocum grunted. "I know you're there."

"You know who isn't here?" Terrance asked. "Bo, James, or Cam. One's in the ground and the other two hightailed it out of here."

"James'll come back."

"Oh, I doubt that. After last night's spectacle, the law

56

will treat them as the menaces they are instead of just some loudmouthed gamblers or workers giving their boss a rough time. When I tried to get anything done the proper way, Bo would put on his best smile and slide right out of it."

"Mmm-hmm."

"I think he may have had something on one of the lawmen around here because you wouldn't believe how relieved he looked when he saw Bo was dead."

"Yeah."

After taking a sip of whiskey, Terrance swirled the dark liquid around in its glass and said, "Then, when Bo stood up and cursed us all for killing him, that's when things really got interesting. Eve had to put a stake through his heart."

"I bet."

"You're not even listening."

"Sure I am," Slocum grunted. "Bo rose up from the dead. Lawmen around here were taking bribes. Same bullshit."

"What if I give you the rest of your payment? It won't be the full amount since I pulled the trigger on Bo, but it'll be enough to compensate you for the fine job you did in winning that battle."

Slocum shifted his stance so he was facing the bar. That way, he could show his face to Terrance while also watching the window from the corner of his eye. "I wouldn't call that a battle. More of a loud disagreement with gunfire involved."

"And a shotgun," Terrance declared proudly. "Don't forget the shotgun."

"I didn't. I was hoping you would before you realized you were the one to end the fight even though you paid me for it."

"You sowed the seeds that set the whole thing up. Aren't you the one who made it look like Bo was turning on them other two?"

"More or less."

"Plus you forced their hand where the threats were concerned. If my men or I had done that, we wouldn't have lived to see it through. Hell, we wouldn't have even made the impression you did when you showed them what's what at the roulette table."

"It wasn't worth what you paid," Slocum said. "I can give back some of the money if you like."

Terrance leaned both elbows on the bar and finished his drink. "Keep it. It'll be earned back anyway at the roulette table Bo left behind and from James's girls."

That caused Slocum to pull his eyes away from the window.

"Yeah," Terrance chuckled. "James forced me to agree on a smaller percentage for the house take on that wheel as well as a smaller percentage of everything coming through here in regards to them girls he was pushing around. I held back a little bit every time to make up for some of what I was losing. Cam was poking his nose through my ledgers, so he would have found out about it in another day or two. Possibly a week if I distracted them some other way."

Slocum grinned and shook his head. "So that's why you were in such a hurry to contact me?"

"Inviting just any hired gun would have set me up to get squeezed in the same vise by another set of hands. Soon as Bo was cleared out, some other scoundrel would have probably taken over his roulette table."

"You're certain of that?"

Terrance and the bartender stared at each other for just a bit too long before finally looking away and getting back to their own sides of the bar. The tender moseyed over to polish some glasses which appeared to be perfectly clean while Terrance picked at a spot in the wood grain that seemed to be doing just fine on its own.

"There was someone else forcing his way into your business before Bo and James, wasn't there?" Slocum asked.

Terrance cleared his throat and impatiently reached over the bar for a bottle.

"More than one?" Slocum inquired.

The theater owner was quick to come to his own defense with "Certainly not!"

"But there was one before Bo?"

"Yes."

"Don't tell me. You hired James to deal with whoever the first one was; he did, and then Bo moved in."

"James just set up shop upstairs. Cam talked him into partnering with Bo."

"But the idea's the same."

"Yes," Terrance replied. "I'm afraid it is."

When Slocum laughed, he didn't exactly know why. It was as if a tired shake of his shoulders just spilled out in the form of a grin and chuckle. Before too long, Terrance had no choice but to join him.

"So you're still worried about James coming back, are you?" Terrance finally asked when he had enough breath to do so.

"Nah. Let him come."

"Good. The way you were watching that window before, I was thinking there might be even more trouble if he did show."

Slocum looked out the window and immediately shifted so he could stare directly outside once again. "He's not the one I was looking for."

"Surely not that dandy you were introducing to the wall?"

"He's a bounty hunter. I don't think too highly of bounty hunters."

"But is he really such a cause for concern?" Terrance asked.

Removing the paper from his pocket, Slocum unfolded it and spread it upon the bar. "This is what concerns me."

After looking at it for all of two seconds, Terrance said, "That's just some poorly scrawled drawing over some words. It's not a proper reward notice, is it?"

"As far as I can tell, no. But it did its job well enough to send one fool after me. If there's one thing I've learned throughout my years on this earth," Slocum growled while pounding a fist against the paper, "it's that there's always more fools to follow the first one into the breach."

"Speaking as a former soldier, I don't think I like those words."

Slocum let out a breath and waggled his empty glass at the barkeep. "Eh, you know what I mean."

When the bartender looked over at Terrance, he got a quick nod to refill the glass. As the drink was poured, Terrance said, "I suppose it's too much to hope that that's the only one that was printed."

Without looking at the notice again, Slocum sighed, "Yeah. Way too much to hope for."

Terrance took the notice by the edge and tugged until Slocum moved his hand. He then leaned against the bar and flapped the notice like it was a newspaper he was straightening so he could read it better. "Real interesting drawing here."

"I noticed."

"Usually there's pictures of the man with the price on his head."

"I know," Slocum snapped.

"And this description . . . very compelling. Almost makes me want to drag you in myself." Seeing the glare from Slocum, Terrance brought a quick end to that line of talk. "Did you really kill eight men in Fort Griffin?"

"No!"

"It ain't out of the question, you know. Maybe they deserved it and there was just some misunderstanding. Maybe it was a long time ago."

"Maybe," Slocum bellowed, "it's a crock of horseshit!"

Clearing his throat and moving another step closer to Slocum, Terrance said, "Could you keep your voice down? My customers are a little skittish after what happened the other night."

"Your customers were more entertained the other night

than when they watch the shows you put on. Come on, Terrance. This is more of a cathouse nailed on top of a saloon than a theater."

"Keep your damn voice down before I have one of my men walk you to the door. After all I did to take the reins back, the last thing I need is for some other asshole with a gun to get ideas when he sees me as a wilting daisy in my own place."

Even though Slocum knew the Stamper guards weren't any sort of a threat, he respected the point Terrance made. It was easy to see one gunman rolling in after the other was ousted, and it was even easier to think that one of those gunmen was keeping a close eye on the theater after what had happened to Bo. Slocum let his shoulders drop back down so they weren't bunched up around his ears, just so he didn't pose a threatening picture. Surprisingly enough, the act felt good in its own right.

"Sorry about that, Terrance. You have been through more than enough without me adding to the mix. Whatever this notice is, it's my problem."

Terrance slipped out of his stern demeanor a few seconds after Slocum let the hairs on the back of his arm settle into place. Looking once again at the notice, he said, "There isn't even a proper sum on this. What self-respecting bounty hunter would bother with such a thing?"

"He wouldn't."

"That man seemed like he could barely fight. Of course, I didn't see much of him, but he wasn't too impressive."

"No," Slocum said as he shifted back around to face Terrance. "He wasn't. You say you've never heard of him?"

"What was his name?"

"Michael Harper."

Terrance only took a few moments to think it over, but Slocum felt like he waited for an hour before the other man finally shook his head and replied, "No. The name doesn't ring any bells. Maybe you should try Braverly."

"Who's that?"

"Not who. Where. Braverly, Illinois." This time, it was Terrance who stared at Slocum as if he were waiting forever for a response. Growing impatient even faster than Slocum had, the older man slapped his hand down on the paper and shoved it toward him. "You should try reading the things on here that don't mention your name. Look right there at the bottom."

"It just goes on about the men that were killed and how—"

"No! The *very* bottom," Terrance said as he stabbed the lowest edge of the paper with his finger. "See?"

If Slocum had been one of those old-timers with a pair of spectacles in his shirt pocket, he would have taken them out and set them on the bridge of his nose. Instead, he was a man who resented the fact that he couldn't see every little thing the first time around. Of course, the tiny letters at the very bottom of the page might very well have been overlooked by a hawk in its prime.

"How the hell did you see that?" Slocum asked as he picked the paper up and brought it closer.

"I'm a businessman, John. If there's anything we need to be aware of, it's fine print."

"So what's this fine print got to do with a notice badmouthing me to anybody who can see it?"

"It's the mark left by the man who printed this. Only reason I recognize it is because he does great work and for a lot less than the printers in Chicago. Come to think of it, I don't even know if there are printers here. I suppose there must be, but . . ." Seeing the impatience building behind Slocum's eyes, Terrance continued, "His name is Ian Carroll. Last I checked, he owned a shop in Braverly."

"And you think he's the one who printed this notice?"

Terrance spread the paper out on the bar so he could run his finger along the print at the bottom. "See this here?

That's the printer's mark. I used Ian's services for all of my advertisements during the Stamper's grand opening and again for a few poker tournaments. It's very important for each printer to sign his work, so to speak. Now that I take a closer look at this, it sure looks like his. See the quality around the edges of the picture?"

Not too eager to look at that picture again, Slocum asked, "What if it's not him? Do you think your printer will be able to figure out whose work this is?"

"Oh, most definitely! Ian's one of the best. If he didn't do this piece himself, he'll know who did. He may have even taught the person everything he knows about the craft. It's not like anyone who buys the equipment can just start cranking out good work like this."

"What kind of records would a printer keep?" Slocum asked before Terrance got too far off on this tangent.

"Beg your pardon?"

"Figuring out who made this piece of trash is one thing," Slocum said while slapping his palm against the rumpled paper. "What I really need to know is who hired him for the job."

Terrance was in his element. The longer he talked about anything related to his business dealings, the straighter he stood. Finally, he grasped one of his lapels like a mayor addressing his constituents. "He should keep records of who commissioned his services, although I couldn't say for certain how willing he'd be to share that information with a stranger."

"He'll do it when he's properly motivated," Slocum growled.

That took a bit of the wind from his sails. "Sure," Terrance said as he snuck a quick look at the Colt Navy hanging at Slocum's side. "I suppose you could go about it that way."

"What else would you suggest?"

"Approach him like a businessman, of course. In fact, I'll vouch for you. We've done enough business in the past that Ian should respect my word on a matter such as this. At least, it could help grease the wheels enough so you won't have to take more drastic measures with a good man like him."

Slocum didn't truly have any intention of riding to a printer's shop just to threaten some poor man with ink on his fingers. Of course, if that notion was enough to get a bit of extra help from Terrance, he was willing to let it ride. "Where's Braverly?"

"Only about two days' ride south of here," Terrance replied. "If you get an early start and ride fast enough, you could make it in about a day and a half. But I'm judging it on when I rode it, which was with a cart, so that could have skewed my estimate somewhat."

"You're awful talkative today, aren't you?"

"Just anxious, I suppose. You don't know what a relief it is to not see Bo behind that wheel of his. And since he's dead without anyone laying claim to his spot, that wheel's mine now. I could stand to make a real good profit."

"Perfect," Slocum said. "What's my percentage?"

A good portion of the eagerness as well as some of the color drained from Terrance's face. He let out a short laugh and patted Slocum's shoulder. "Almost got me there."

"Don't you think it's fair for me to get a percentage of one table after the risk I took? You wouldn't even have that table all to yourself if it wasn't for me."

"I . . . suppose."

"Tell you what. I'll settle for a good horse and some gear for the ride to Braverly."

"A good horse is worth a pretty penny."

"How much is it worth to you for me to swing by here again and make my presence known to discourage any other gunmen looking to fill Bo's spot?" Spotting a hint of concern in the other man's eyes, Slocum added, "You're the one who told me about the dangers of leaving yourself open to enterprising gunmen like . . . well . . . like those men over there by Bo's table."

Terrance turned so quickly that he almost made a spark with his boots scraping against the floor. The theater wasn't full by any means, but there were several men in the place. Most of them were playing cards at their own tables and a few were talking to the girls working the main floor. Two, however, were idly circling the table where Bo's roulette wheel sat under a white tarp. They talked among themselves and nodded, but were too far away for Terrance to hear them.

"I can frighten them off before I leave," Slocum said, "but after I leave . . ."

"When you stop by again, stay for a week or so and you've got a deal."

Odds were that those men at the roulette table were simply talking about Bo's messy departure from the theater. Before Terrance saw past his nervousness to realize that, Slocum extended a hand and said, "You've got a deal."

8

The ride from Chicago had taken even less time than
Terrance had promised. The horse Terrance had given him
wasn't the finest in his small collection, but it was strong
and young enough to have plenty of spirit in him. It was a
fine animal with a tan coat and dark patches along his left
side. As soon as it had put Chicago behind it, the horse had
been reluctant to slow down. Slocum arrived in the little
town too late to get a hot supper, but just in time to rent a
room before the owner of the town's only hotel stopped
answering his door.

Early the next morning, Slocum got started with a breakfast of watery eggs and burned toast. The food was just something to fill his belly, and he washed it down with enough
coffee to do the trick. Unable to get any good information
from anyone at the hotel, Slocum struck out on his own to
explore Braverly. It didn't take long.

The town was arranged to look larger than it truly was.

66

Whether this had been done on purpose or not, Slocum couldn't say. What he did know was that the sharply winding streets made it difficult to see from one end to another. Carts had to be driven at a snail's pace to navigate the turns, which slowed things down even more for the few folks who needed to use the streets. Because Slocum had put his horse up in a stable, he could cut across those streets, duck into alleys, and even cut through a general store to cover more ground. All that running gave him some exercise, but not a lot of results. In the end, he found the printer's shop he'd been seeking purely by accident.

It was a large structure that had the look of an old barn, on the outskirts of town. A sign hanging above the two large main doors bore Ian Carroll's name. The doors, however, were boarded up. Slocum quickly spotted a regular-sized door that had been sawed into the wall near the corner of the building. It was propped open, by a bucket filled with broken printing tiles of all sizes, to let the stench of ink, grease, and wood pulp drift outside.

Slocum knocked on the door and stuck his nose inside. "Hello? Anyone here?"

"Yes," someone called from deep inside the old barn.

"Mr. Carroll? Are you here?"

"Yes, yes!"

Stepping inside, Slocum took in the sight of two large presses. Each machine took up a good portion of its half of the room. The sound of metal clanking against metal rattled up to the converted loft, but he couldn't quite pin down its source. Slocum took a few more steps inside and asked, "Can I have a word with Ian Carroll?"

"I told you— OW!"

The exclamation was punctuated by the sound of something much softer than metal knocking against one of the printing presses. A tall, gangly man dressed in a blacksmith's apron and a gun belt stood up next to the press on Slocum's right. Seeing the holster at the other man's hip,

Slocum's hand reflexively drifted toward the Colt Navy at his side. When the tall man in the apron staggered sideways while rubbing the top of his head, it became clear that there was no gun in his holster. Instead, several tools were stuffed in where a firearm should have been, and stayed put thanks to the stitching that sealed the bottom of the holster.

"I'm Ian Carroll," the tall man said. As he rubbed his head again, he winced and moved his hand down to get a look at the little bit of blood smeared on his fingers. "Oh, that's going to sting for a while. What can I do for you?"

Slocum walked forward and reached into his jacket pocket for a thin envelope. "My name's . . ." Stifling the reflex to introduce himself properly, Slocum decided to skip over his name for now. Considering the nature of his visit, it may not be wise to be the man thought of as a cold-blooded murderer. "I'm here on behalf of Terrance Pinder."

"Terrance, eh? What'd you say your name was again?"

"My name's John. Here you go," Slocum said with a smile as he handed the envelope to the printer. "This should explain things."

Ian took the envelope, opened it, and then unfolded the letter within. Slocum's name wasn't on that letter either, but Terrance had been careful to word it so as not to make that omission seem suspicious. Even so, Ian seemed more than a little suspicious when he shifted his bloodshot green eyes toward the man in front of him. "And who might you be?"

Sighing as he weighed his options, Slocum decided the truth was his best bet. If anything, instilling a bit of nervousness in the printer might just shake something loose that he wouldn't have gotten before. "I'm John Slocum."

At first, Slocum was glad to see only a subtle shift in the other man's expression. Within seconds, it became clear that the shift was from a twinge of pain on the top of Ian's head. When nothing else came of the revelation, Slocum became a little confused.

"Do you recognize the name?" Slocum asked.

"I think I do. Was it from one of the advertisements I printed up for Terrance?"

"No."

"Oh, now I think I recall! It was for that banner I made for Mr. Corrington! You'll have to excuse me. I knocked my head while tending to one of my sick girls over there, and my eyeballs are still rattlin'. Come on in and make yourself comfortable while I clean myself up."

Slocum followed Ian all the way to the back of what he could clearly see was indeed an old barn. Supplies were stored overhead in a reinforced loft. Machinery was sectioned off in what used to be animal stalls, and paper was stacked high in the same spot where hay bales would have been kept. In what may have been a horse stall or possibly a spot to park a small cart, Ian had set up an office. The polished desk and clean table looked mighty peculiar situated in a place that still smelled of manure. The tall man went to the desk, took a folded handkerchief from a drawer, and pressed it against his bleeding scalp.

"Terrance wrote some nice things about you in that letter," Ian said. "I assume this is for some sort of large job?"

"More like for a job you've already done." Slocum removed the notice from his pocket. By now, the paper was folded in several different spots and rumpled to the point of looking more like old cheesecloth. Ian gazed upon it as if he was looking at an illuminated manuscript.

"Ahh yes. Just as I'd thought. You are that John Slocum."

Still prepared for a bad reaction, Slocum was now positively flummoxed. "So you do recognize this?"

"Most definitely! I can't speak for the quality of the material as depicted in the drawing, but printing several copies of such detailed work in such a short amount of time is quite a feat. You can see for yourself, it turned out very well indeed."

"Did you read what this is?"

"Most assuredly. That's not part of my job, but I read

about everything I can get my hands on. It's a love of the printed word, you see. Surely not much of a surprise for a man in my line of work."

"The man who carried this tried to shoot me," Slocum explained. "He was a bounty hunter who thought I killed eight men in Fort Griffin."

"What's his name?"

"Michael Harper."

Ian's eyes rolled up, down, and around in their sockets as if his next thought was etched somewhere on the walls surrounding his desk. Since there wasn't anything up there but cobwebs and the spiders that had spun them, he quickly looked back to Slocum. "Should I recognize that name?"

"He's one of the men who carried a notice that you printed. The one you're holding, in fact."

"Where was he?"

"He tracked me down from Chicago, but he could have come from somewhere else."

"I certainly hope so," Ian said. "Chicago isn't that far away. Now, if you'd told me he came from New York, or possibly overseas, with one of my pieces, that would be impressive. I don't know if anything I've printed has ever made it that far."

"This thing you printed nearly got me shot," Slocum snapped.

"Really?"

"Yes! It paints me as some kind of damn monster! Look at the picture for Christ's sake! That's supposed to be me standing over a pile of dead bodies!"

Ian looked at the picture but didn't seem to think much of it. When he looked at Slocum, he was shaking his head and allowing his mouth to hang open as if he didn't know which words to form.

"Who's Mr. Corrington?" Slocum asked.

Recoiling as if he'd been smacked on the nose, Ian blinked

a few more times and sputtered, "He's . . . he's the one who commissioned the piece. That piece. The one you say . . . well . . ."

"Ahh. Now we're getting somewhere. Who is he?"

"He wrote it."

"You already said as much. Why did he write it?"

Now Ian seemed to be so confused that his brain actually hurt. Before popping a spring in his head, he went to his desk and sat on a little chair. Lowering his head allowed him to dab at the wound with his handkerchief before any more blood trickled down his face. "He did write the notice, but that's not what I meant." Quickly glancing down at the paper, he found one of the top lines and tapped it with his finger. "There. See? That's what he wrote."

Slocum looked at what Ian had showed him. "'*Six-Gun Devil*'? He came up with that?"

"Along with the rest, but . . . Aww this is getting to be too much for me."

"Why's that so special?"

"That's the name of the book."

That caused a rush of cold to roll beneath Slocum's skin. "What book?" he asked.

"The book right there. *Six-Gun Devil*. He wrote it."

"And you printed it?"

"No," Ian sighed. He kept his eyes closed while pressing the clean side of the handkerchief against them. That way, he could at least sit on his chair without wobbling. "That's just an advertisement for the book. Did you even really speak with Terrance Pinder? Didn't he tell you that I print advertisements?"

"Yeah, he did tell me that, but I thought . . . Oh, never mind what I thought. You got another chair around here?"

"Over there," he said while waving toward what had definitely once been an animal's stall.

Slocum walked to the stall and could only find a milking

stool. It seemed strong enough to support his weight, so he
brought it closer to Ian's desk and sat on it. "So *Six-Gun
Devil* is a book?"

"Yes."

"What kind of book?"

"The kind folks buy and read. What sort of question is
that?"

"It's a book about something that happened in Fort Griffin?" Slocum asked with as much patience as he could
dredge up.

"I guess so. He gave me a copy, but I haven't read it."

Slocum leaned forward, rubbing his hands together.
"You've got a copy? Can I see it?"

"I suppose." Ian stood up and wiped his brow with the
back of his hand. After what appeared to be a bout with
dizziness, he placed both hands on his hips and looked
around with renewed vigor. "Where did I put that book?"

"What about any records you have regarding Mr. Corrington? Can I see those?"

"No, most certainly not. My records are my business."

Slocum let the matter lie. He could always come back to
it later. Right now, it was more important to try and make a
little bit of progress after all of the messing about he'd been
forced to endure just to converse with the printer.

Ian moved slowly at first, but quickly gained speed, until
he was like a giant horsefly buzzing from one spot to another. Every so often, he would stand in one spot and toss
some things around before muttering and buzzing somewhere else. Somehow, even after all of his rummaging, the
shop didn't look any messier. Slocum couldn't make sense
of all the machinery and supplies before, and he couldn't
now. After a while, Slocum couldn't even stay angry at the
other man or the situation. It was just too amusing to watch
Ian dart about the converted barn, banging his knees against
the presses, smacking his arms against various posts, and

accidentally poking his wound while trying to scratch his head. The icing on the cake was that his entire tour of his own shop wound up with him about two steps away from where he'd started.

"Just one more place to look, I suppose," Ian grumbled as he began pulling open his desk drawers one by one. Of course, it wasn't until he'd dug to the bottom of the last drawer that he triumphantly declared, "Found it!"

The book wasn't very big and its pages were all curled at the edges, as if it had been left out in the sun after a rainstorm. Taking it to get a look for himself, Slocum gripped the book so it was as flat as he could make it. That way, he could more easily see the picture on the front. While it wasn't identical to the one on the notice, the depiction on the cover didn't appear any more flattering for the man labeled as the *Six-Gun Devil*.

"This is just one of them trashy books people leave on trains," Slocum said.

"I'd never leave this on a train!" Ian said as if Slocum had just insulted his youngest daughter. "If it's anything like his others, it's got to be damn good."

"Got to be? So you haven't read it?"

"No, but I stand by what I advertise."

Talking to Ian was starting to give Slocum a headache. Rather than make it worse, he flipped the book open to start leafing through the pages. Slocum didn't get a chance to absorb the whole thing, but he saw his own name mentioned several times, along with enough shooting and death to fill a small war. "This is complete bullshit," he grumbled.

"Don't blame me. Blame the writer," Ian countered.

"I thought you stood by what you advertise."

That one snuck beneath Ian's guard. He winced and gnawed on the inside of his cheek with genuine contemplation. Finally, he asked, "You're really a friend of Terrance's?"

"Didn't you read the letter?"

Slocum put the odds of that holding any water at about fifty-fifty. Fortunately for him, the coin landed with the right side up.

"I suppose it's not a big secret," Ian said. "There's been other men asking to meet Mr. Corrington, so you might as well know too."

"Know what?"

"He's coming by my shop sometime in the next few days."

"Mr. Corrington?" Slocum asked as he hopped to his feet. "The same man who wrote this book?"

"The one and only."

"What's he coming back for?"

"I don't know yet, do I?" Ian replied in a huff. "He can't tell me until he gets here!"

More than anything, Slocum wanted to storm out of there and not come back until he had someone to shoot. But more questions came to mind, and Ian seemed to be in an answering frame of mind, so he asked, "What did you do with these advertisements once you printed them?"

"Handed them out as much as I could, but it's not my job to circulate them."

"Whose job is it?"

"I pay boys to do some running, hand them off to stage-coach drivers when they come through town, send a few bundles to bigger towns like Chicago and such. After that, it's anyone's guess. Mr. Corrington is coming up in his profession, so I'd assume he's awfully good at spreading word of his books around. From what I've heard, they're very popular in the southern regions."

"Yeah," Slocum grunted. "I'd like to place my boot in this Corrington fella's southern region."

"What was that?"

"Nothing. What were you saying about the South?"

"Just that his books come up from down there and spread like wildfire. At least they did according to this."

When he said that last part, Ian gazed down at the advertisement he'd printed with the unbridled pride of a father watching his son become President of the United States. "For all I know, my work may very well have gotten all the way to New York by now."

"When's he coming back?"

"Sometime in the next few days. A busy man like him must have a lot on his plate. Would you like me to try and arrange a meeting?"

"No," Slocum replied. "I'll see to it myself."

9

Slocum picked a spot across the street from the printer's barn where he could kick his feet up and wait for the rest of the day.

After a short supper, he waited some more.

He spent a few hours of restless sleep in a rented bed that was somehow angled so his feet were higher than his head no matter which end he chose for his pillow. After a breakfast consisting of oatmeal that tasted more like brick mortar, he returned to his spot and waited.

The whole day dragged by as he continued to watch . . . and wait.

Some locals caught sight of him, but only shook their heads the way they might at a transient who'd wandered in from somewhere to lie in a ditch for a while. Slocum watched Ian come and go from his shop, but the printer was too wrapped up in whatever he was doing to notice anything beyond the tip of whatever tool was in his hand at the time.

The sun dipped below the horizon and still Slocum waited.

It was a chilly September night, which would have felt

good under normal circumstances. With all the waiting he'd been doing, Slocum felt more like he'd spent the last month sitting in that increasingly uncomfortable spot, looking at an old barn as the world slowly turned around him. He was getting so tired that he had nearly dozed off when he finally spotted something he'd been hoping to see.

Someone was approaching the barn and it wasn't Ian.

Slocum swung his feet down from the old section of fence he'd been using and leaned forward for a better look. It was a man dressed in simple clothes, including a vest buttoned up beneath a well-worn jacket. Even in the fading sunlight, Slocum could tell the chain crossing the man's stomach wasn't connected to a valuable watch. Nobody who could afford something like that would wear a rumpled jacket or pants that were so frayed around the edges. His hat was flat on top and had a wide brim that cast a thick shadow over his clean-shaven face.

Once the other man put his back to Slocum so he could approach the door of the printing shop, Slocum quickened his pace to get to him. The closer he got, the more he wanted to draw his Colt and knock some sense into the author of *Six-Gun Devil*. He thought of plenty of things he wanted to say regarding the damage the book had done, and when he closed in to arm's reach of the writer, Slocum had to force himself to hold back before giving in to his more sinister instincts.

Slocum drew a breath so he could introduce himself, but wasn't able to get one word out before the man in front of him wheeled around and hit him with a set of knuckles that cracked solidly against his jaw.

"There you are, asshole!" the man snarled through a mouth that curled into a vicious grin. As he lunged at Slocum, his jacket opened to reveal the gun belt strapped around his waist.

Slocum was surprised by the punch, but reacted quickly enough to duck away from the follow-up. Of the two, that was the swing to avoid, because that fist was wrapped around the handle of a Bowie knife. The sharpened steel sliced through the air directly in front of Slocum's throat, stopped a few feet away, and was swung right back at him again. Slocum raised his right arm just in time to block a swing that would have surely carved him like a Christmas goose.

After pushing the man's knife hand away, Slocum drove a fist straight into his face. The impact sent a ripple of pain through his forearm but felt very rewarding considering who was on the receiving end of it.

Shaking off the punch and then spitting on the ground, the other man ducked beneath Slocum's left hook to slash at his midsection. The knife tore through a section of Slocum's shirt but barely scraped against flesh. Slocum hopped back and then reached down to grab hold of the man's wrist. Once he had some degree of control over where the blade was headed next, Slocum took a moment to assess the situation.

The other man was just a little shorter than him and knew how to use his knife. The gun he carried looked like a .44 and didn't seem like something bought for show. He was a strong one, too. Slocum could only hang onto the man's wrist for a few more seconds before it was ripped free of his grasp.

"Oh, no," the man grunted. "You ain't gettin' off that light."

Before Slocum could respond, he saw the knife come at him again. It whistled past his face and came across in the opposite direction at chest level. That second swing clipped a section of Slocum's jacket, cutting through as if it was a sheet of paper from Ian's shop.

"Are you Mr. Corrington?" Slocum asked.

Hearing that name brought a snarl to the man's lips, and he came at Slocum again. This time, he made a quick feinting stab to draw Slocum's arms down before taking a quick swing at shoulder level. The blade sliced through a good section of meat, spraying Slocum's blood onto the ground. Just as he was recovering from that, Slocum saw the man lunge in for another stab.

Slocum was barely quick enough to cross his arms at the wrists and drop them down to divert the blade before it was buried hilt-deep into his gut. He then twisted to one side and closed his hands around the man's wrist like a set of pincers. A sharp twist and forceful grab allowed him to relieve the man of his weapon. Slocum spun around to face him, and found nothing but empty space. Suddenly, an arm snaked around his neck from behind and a fist pounded against his ribs.

"How you like that?" the man snarled into Slocum's ear. "Not so good, is it? Well it's about to get a whole lot worse."

Rather than try to get out of the man's grip, Slocum placed a hand on the arm encircling his neck, to hold it in place. The punches kept coming, each one landing in the same spot, until his ribs felt like broken glass scraping against his innards. Slocum leaned forward until he lifted the other man off his feet and then charged backward into a nearby tree.

The other man let out a grunt and let go of Slocum's neck. The punches kept coming, however, even after Slocum turned around to face him.

In an attempt to bring a quick end to the fight, Slocum drew his Colt. He hadn't intended on shooting, but he didn't even get a chance to aim the gun before it was knocked out of his hand.

"You wanna step this up, do ya?" the other man snarled. "Well I can do that just fine."

"Aw hell," Slocum grunted as he saw the man reach for his pistol.

The gun was indeed a .44. Slocum got a real good look at it because he ran forward to close the distance between him and the other man before the trigger could be pulled. Half a second before the .44 went off, Slocum had a solid hold on the man's arm, and he twisted until the pistol dropped to the ground a few inches from where he'd tossed the knife.

Rather than try to retrieve his weapon, the man slapped both hands against Slocum's back, grabbed onto his clothing, and rammed Slocum into the same tree he'd hit a few moments ago. Slocum barely had enough time to turn his head and twist his body around before he could be knocked into oblivion. Even so, it was a long way from a tickle when he hit that standing timber.

The man stood in front of him wearing a crooked smile on his bloodied face. That sight alone gave Slocum the incentive to start chopping away at him as if he was bringing down the tree that had bruised half his body. His fists thumped against layers of tensed muscle in a quick series of blows. Although the first couple didn't do much, the ones immediately after them caught the man's attention. As soon as Slocum felt the man take half a step back, he delivered a powerful uppercut to his chin.

The man's head snapped back, but he took the punch a lot better than Slocum had anticipated. In fact, when he craned his neck back around to look at him, he was still smiling. "That's gonna make it all the sweeter when I drop you on your tenderfoot ass."

"Tenderfoot?" Slocum snarled as he rocked the man with a right cross that was so quick there was no time to brace for it. "Better watch where you're directing a name like that, boy."

His face twisting into something uglier than before, the man growled, "Boy? Is that what you just called me?" Uninterested in Slocum's reply, he lowered his shoulder and charged at him like a bull.

Slocum wanted to step aside and let the man run past him, but he caught the man's shoulder on the ribs that hadn't been tenderized by punches already. It would have been less painful for him to have just held his ground and taken what was headed his way. A sharp pain lanced up through Slocum's torso like a hand, to reach into his lungs and steal his next breath. He allowed his body to go limp as he struggled to suck in some more wind.

"Is somebody out here?" Ian called from his shop as the door creaked open. Although Slocum didn't bother looking toward the printer, he could hear a few surprised sounds come out of him as he caught sight of the scuffle taking place just a few yards away from his doorstep.

Still being driven back, Slocum dug one boot into the dirt behind him to bring both himself and the other man to a jarring halt. He then drove that same leg forward until his knee pounded against the other man's hip. It wasn't much more than a wild, glancing blow, but it bought him some breathing room.

"Stay outta this, old man!" the fellow in front of Slocum roared. "This is between me and the writer!"

"Writer?" Slocum asked in between gulps for air.

"That's right. I know who you are. And I bet you don't even know who you're lookin' at."

"Actually I don't."

Lowering his stance so his shoulders were slouched forward and his head was low, the man looked as if he was about to run at Slocum on all fours as he said, "Daniel Sykes. Bet you wish you hadn't come around here tonight, huh?"

"Never heard of you. But I'm not a writer, either," Slocum replied. "I think we've got ourselves a bit of a misunderstanding."

"The hell we do!" Without waiting for another moment, Sykes ran at Slocum just as he'd advertised. When he got within a few feet, he extended both arms to corral him in the event Slocum attempted to dodge to either side.

Slocum twisted sideways and lifted his arms so they wouldn't get wrapped up in the other man's grasp. While Sykes churned up dirt with both feet and tried to lock his arms around him, Slocum clasped his hands together and dropped them like a hammer on Sykes's back. He had enough time to pick his shot this time, and he hit the man's spine dead on. Grunting in pain, Sykes was barely able to remain upright as his arms instinctively pulled in closer to protect his body. That set him up nicely for another well-placed blow.

Then, Slocum backed away until his boot touched the .44 that had been dropped. Scooping up the pistol, he asked, "Who the hell are you, Daniel Sykes?"

"You sayin' you ain't heard of me? Then why the hell were you waiting for me to come along?"

"I wasn't waiting for you." Thumbing back the hammer of the .44 made a loud metallic click that did a good job of catching Sykes's attention. "I'm only asking you once more before I assume the worst. Who the hell are you?"

Rather than test Slocum's resolve, he said, "I'm from as far south as the Arizona Territories, but I've done some work in Kansas, Wyoming, and up into the Dakotas."

"What kind of work?"

"He's a cattle driver," Ian said as he approached them. "I spoke to him earlier, Mr. Slocum. He's just a good fella who does odd jobs wherever he can find 'em. Used to be the same way myself before I found my calling and got my presses together. However this started, it doesn't have to end any worse. Everyone just take a breath and settle down."

Despite having been knocked around and riled up, Sykes looked like a man who was in his element. He wore a devil's grin and even winked at Slocum when he said, "That's right. Ain't no need for this to get any worse."

"Aren't you forgetting that you're the one who came at me first?" Slocum said.

"Only because you were lurking like some kinda ghoul in the shadows."

"I assure you, Mr. Slocum is no ghoul," Ian said. "He was probably just coming to have another word with me regarding Mr. Corrington's visit. Isn't that right, Mr. Slocum?"

Sykes twitched several times throughout that short response. It seemed several things Ian was talking about had piqued his interest. "You're John Slocum?"

"That's right."

Finally, Sykes shifted his stance so he didn't look like he was ready to attack. "Well then. We might have somethin' in common after all."

"Like what?"

"Like wantin' to have a talk with a certain writer in regards to some yellowback novels."

10

The saloon was a long structure with a high ceiling full of
birds that had made their nests up in the rafters. Tables were
arranged in a manner that allowed customers to pull their
chairs out while also avoiding the white stains where bird
shit had fallen from above. Basically one large room with
the front door at one end and the bar at the other, it was a
place that felt more spacious on the inside than it looked on
the outside. Having noticed the bird dung on the floor, Slocum had been quick to pick his seat first when he, Sykes,
and Ian had gotten a table.

Ever the gentleman, Ian had made the long walk to the
bar to fetch the first round of drinks. That gave Slocum and
Sykes a few moments to speak privately.

"Let me guess," Sykes said. "You found your name
smeared all over some book that ain't good enough to wipe
yer ass with?"

"Something like that."

"The book was written by Edward Corrington?"

"Sounds about right."

Pressing both hands down on the table, Sykes once again

looked more like an animal stalking toward him than like a man. "That's the same asshole that wrote about me."

"What did he write about you?"

"Never you mind. All that's important is that he spread enough lies to enough folks that I got chased out of two different towns for doing nothin' more than riding in and trying to get myself fed."

"Somehow, I get the feeling you're used to getting into trouble," Slocum said.

Sykes leaned away and shifted his hat so it rested on the back of his head. "I ain't no saint, but neither are you. What did you intend on doing to that little shit writer when you got your hands on him?"

"Never you mind."

"That's what I thought," Sykes chuckled. He looked toward the back of the room, where Ian was paying for the drinks. As the printer did his best to carry them all to the table, Sykes said, "I know where to find that writer, but he won't be here for long."

"How do you know? You haven't even laid eyes on him."

"And how would you know such a thing?"

"Because you thought I was him when we first crossed paths," Slocum pointed out.

"It was dark." After a few seconds of bearing the brunt of Slocum's gaze, Sykes admitted, "I seen him in passing, and I can tell you he already passed right on outta this town."

"I suppose you'll want me to go chasing after him?"

"Nah," Sykes replied as Ian got close enough for the clink of the glasses in his hands to be heard. "I thought we'd both go after him."

That was still settling in the back of Slocum's head when Ian sat down and spilled about a quarter of the beer he'd brought with him. "I see you two haven't killed each other while I was away," the printer said. "That's good."

"Not yet, we haven't," Slocum muttered.

"Yes, well . . . still good. I thought we could all do with a drink, so this round's my treat." Raising his mug, Ian said, "Here's to misunderstandings and the good friends that come from them."

"Let's not push it," Slocum replied.

All this time, Sykes kept his wolfish grin intact and his eyes fixed on Slocum. Obviously sizing the other man up, he seemed to like what he was seeing so far. After taking a long pull from his beer, he slammed the mug down and wiped his mouth with the back of his hand. "Not bad at all! If I'd known I'd get some free beer out of it, I would've walked into that ambush sooner. So what would've happened if Johnny Boy would have shot me? Free steak dinner?"

"Maybe we can find out," Slocum warned.

Even though nobody else in the saloon seemed to take much notice of them, Ian scooted forward and fidgeted as if they were on center stage. "Let's not get hasty, gentlemen. As I've explained a dozen times on the way over here, this was nothing but a misunderstanding. I'm sure the fact that you two seem so set on harming Mr. Corrington is probably some grave error as well." Seeing the glares he got from both other men at the table, Ian quickly amended his statement with "Or maybe not. Either way, he doesn't seem to be here, so you two don't have any reason to fight."

After giving Ian a quick nod, Sykes stretched a hand across the table, which also forced him to drag his sleeve through the pool of spilled beer Ian had left. "He's right. We don't got no reason to tear each other's throats out."

"I suppose not," Slocum grudgingly admitted.

"Well that's good enough for me," Ian declared. "Cheers!"

The three of them completed the toast in the most unbalanced way possible. Sykes extended his mug as far out as he could toward Slocum, who held his up just to get it to his mouth, while Ian made the rounds by knocking his mug enthusiastically against the other two. In the end, there was more beer spilled on them and the table than whatever managed to get into any mouths.

"So," Sykes said in a voice that was a stark contrast to the vaguely cordial tone he'd used before, "where the hell is Mr. Corrington anyway?"

"I honestly don't know," Ian replied. "He was supposed to come to town to commission another piece of work, but it wasn't set in stone. I may get my instructions through the mail, or he might even deliver them at a later date. Considering his rising success, I'd wager you'll see the fruits of our labors soon enough."

"When was the last time you heard from him?" Slocum asked.

"I received a telegram about two weeks ago. Said he was in St. Louis receiving some sort of accolade or possibly researching a new book. He meant to head up to Chicago and was going to meet with me along the way. I figured he should have arrived by today, but I could be wrong. If anything went wrong with his travel arrangements or if he was delayed on account of his publishing commitments, his schedule could be very much askew."

"Very much askew," Sykes said. "That's one way of describing him."

Slocum couldn't help but laugh when he heard that. Judging by the look on Ian's face, you'd think he'd just arranged for a treaty the likes of which no war had ever seen.

"There now!" the older man said. "That's more like it. Who wants another beer?"

Since Ian was buying, neither man was going to refuse.

It turned out that Ian could hold his liquor. It may have been a result of all the ink he'd inhaled on a daily basis, but the older man's system was hardened more than the sides of his printing presses. Slocum, on the other hand, was barely steady enough to walk out of the saloon without knocking anything over.

The night air did him a world of good, hitting him like a cold slap across both cheeks. He stood in the shadows pouring out from the alley with his hands on his hips and his chin held up to catch a passing breeze. The air smelled of burning wood and impending rain. It was the scent of autumn and was a welcome change from the odors filling a saloon that was packed full of drunken men. When the door swung open and slammed shut, Slocum didn't need more than one guess to figure out who was staggering toward him. Ian had already left, and the locals mostly headed for the street instead of the mouth of a dark alley.

"So what do you say, Johnny?"

"First of all," Slocum replied as he turned to look at Sykes, "if you call me Johnny again, I'll finish what I started outside of Ian's barn."

"And second?"

"Second, if you ever call me Johnny *Boy* again, I'll shoot you where you stand."

Sykes held up both hands and showed him a sloppy grin. "I was just needlin' you is all. I meant to ask you about what you thought in regards to the proposition I made a while ago. The one where—"

"I know the one," Slocum interrupted.

"Well? What do you think?"

"I've had men come after me before. Sometimes it's a genuine concern and sometimes it's a mistake. This was just one bounty hunter who didn't have his head screwed on right. If I spent my time chasing down every one of those, I wouldn't have time for much else."

"And where's that bounty hunter now?" Sykes asked.

"Last I saw him was in Chicago. Once things went bad there, he hightailed it out of my sight and I haven't seen him since."

Nodding, Sykes hitched his thumbs over his belt and moseyed away from the alley. After three or four steps, he stopped and glanced over his shoulder. "That bounty hunter wouldn't have been a long-faced dandy with a bowler hat, would he?"

Slocum's eyes narrowed, but he didn't say a word.

Apparently, Sykes wasn't drunk enough to miss that signal, because he pounced on it like a hawk diving to scoop up a field mouse. "Could his name have been Mike Harper?"

Whatever haze had been in Slocum's head was cleared out when he heard that question. Standing up a bit straighter, he asked, "What do you know about him?"

"Just that he's more than some bounty hunter. He's from out east. Maybe some big-time law dog."

"He sure didn't act like one. I doubt he's even shot a man."

"Appearances can be deceiving, Johnny B . . . er . . . John. Harper's the sort who doesn't give up a trail so easily. He came after me for a while when I had my first bout of trouble from Corrington's books. It took a hell of a lot to shake him then, and the only reason I did is because he sank his teeth into someone else."

"I know about that all too well. My head's starting to hurt, so I think I'm gonna crawl into bed."

As Slocum started walking, Sykes fell into step right beside him. "That Harper fella takes every word Corrington writes as gospel, and he ain't the only one. Unless someone puts a stop to that writer, he's gonna keep cranking out those books until neither of us can get a moment's peace. Wait too long and it'll be too late to do anything about it. These things get a momentum of their own, you know. Like a rock rollin' straight down the side of a—"

Sykes stopped short when Slocum came to an abrupt halt in the middle of the street. A cart drawn by a single horse clattered toward them, so both men moved onto the boardwalk.

"So tell me," Slocum said. "What was written about you that's got you so worked up?"

"It was a goddamn yellowback novel like the one you're in."

"Like the one I'm in? So it's not the same one."

"Didn't you read it?"

"Not yet," Slocum grunted. "But I get the impression that you've read yours. Must be one hell of a yarn."

"It was . . ." Pausing long enough to glance suspiciously up and down the street, Sykes dropped his voice to a snarling whisper. "It was called *The Gentleman Killer*. Says I snuck into rich folks' houses and slit their throats while they was sleepin'. What kind of cowardly bullshit is that? No matter how many times I read it, I still couldn't even figure out if I was supposed to be the gentleman or if those were the assholes I was supposed to have cut. What's so goddamn funny?"

Letting his head hang as he kept laughing, Slocum replied, "I'm just wondering how much this writer would pay to see us get so flustered about all of this. Forget about Ian's banners, this is some damn good advertising."

"It's soiling my good name, that's what it is. Yours too, so I don't got a clue why you're so damn cheery all of a sudden."

"It strikes me that we both got our feathers rubbed the wrong way over some bullshit that was said about us. Haven't you ever had some nasty gossip thrown around about you?"

"Sure I have. Know what I did about it? I found whoever was gossiping and made them sorry they ever opened their fucking mouths."

"Yeah, well maybe we should both learn to turn the other cheek."

"This coming from a man who came all the way down here from Chicago to beat the tar out of a writer?"

"Perhaps we should both find something else to do with our time. If you wanna work so hard to help spread the word about a bunch of books that aren't worth the paper they're printed on, go right ahead. Maybe that Corrington fella will give you a cut of the profits."

When Slocum walked away, Sykes stayed put. "You're making a mistake, Slocum! Men like us can't afford to let bullshit like this pass! First it's a fancy-pants like Harper coming after us, but more will follow. We'll be seen as weak!"

"I don't give a damn what people see," Slocum called back.

"You're just gonna let Harper get away with coming after you? If you get sick of letting that writer get away with draggin' us through the mud, you can find me at the Creek House Saloon!"

As Slocum kept walking toward his hotel, he laid odds on whether or not Sykes would come rushing after him. The closer he got to the corner, the likelier it seemed that he wouldn't be through with the other man just yet. Then, after he rounded the corner, the odds slipped further and further down, until he'd written off the possibility altogether. Sykes shouted a few things after him, but that was it. When he had stepped into his hotel and felt the cold winds get cut off by the slam of the front door, Slocum was ready to put the whole thing behind him.

The woman behind the front desk was a stout redhead with full lips and teeth that were just a little too big for her face. She had a pretty smile, however, which she showed him the moment he approached the desk. "I was just about to lock up for the night. Glad I didn't."

"Me too. I need the key to my room."

She let her eyes wander along the front of Slocum's shirt as her fingers drifted across the laces keeping the front of her blouse closed. The chill from outside had apparently blown in ahead of Slocum because her nipples were hard and pressing against the material. Lowering her eyes as if she'd felt him looking at her, she turned and walked to the peg board nailed to the wall behind the counter holding the hotel's ledger. Loose, dark brown skirts twirled around her, brushing against wide hips and a backside that Slocum could easily imagine in his hands.

"Busy day?"

"What was that?" Slocum asked as he forced his eyes to head north of her waistline.

She took a key from its hook, turned around, and held it as if she didn't have any intention of handing it over. "I asked if you had a busy day. Haven't seen you since breakfast."

"Oh, right. Yeah. It's been a hell of a day."

"I could draw you a hot bath. Just say the word and I'll start warming up some water."

"No need for all that trouble. Think I'll just get some sleep."

"No trouble. If you like, I could even make sure your back gets scrubbed nice and clean."

He looked at her again, studying her eyes and the promising smile that remained etched onto her soft, moist lips. "Would that cost more than the price of a room?"

"Not for you."

Reaching out to take the key she offered, Slocum replied, "Then I don't see how I could refuse."

"Good," she told him while walking around the desk to check the front door. "I'm Kate, by the way."

"You need help bringing a tub to my room, or do you have somewhere else in mind?"

"I've already got it ready. All I need to do is boil some water to warm it up."

11

Slocum's room was barely large enough for him to walk around the bed without knocking into something. The only other furnishings, a rickety chair and a three-legged table just big enough for a pocket watch and some coins, had been moved into a corner to make room for a metal wash tub. Actually, calling the oversized pail a tub was being generous. It had the long, oval shape of a tub, but it hardly seemed big enough for one man to get in and sit down. The tub was only slightly wider than Slocum's hips and so short that the edge barely pressed against the portion of his back a few inches below his armpits. When he stripped and stepped into the cool water, a portion of it sloshed over the sides and onto one of the towels that had been laid on the floor.

Kate walked in a few minutes later, carrying a steaming kettle and wearing a long robe that hung open to give him a good look at the naked body beneath it. Her curves were even better than he'd expected, and she carried herself as if she enjoyed showing them off. Plump breasts swayed beneath the robe and her hair had been loosed from the ribbons that had previously held it up. Her tongue darted out to run along her lips as she sat on the edge of the tub and poured the hot water.

"There," she purred. "Is that better?"

"Much," Slocum replied, even before the water had a chance to warm up what had already been in the tub. He reached out to move her robe aside so he could see the creamy skin of her hips and the soft slope of her belly. Slocum looked up at her face while easing his hand south to the downy hair between her legs.

Kate closed her eyes and shuddered when his fingers found the lips of her pussy.

"Seems like I'm not the only one that's wet," he teased.

If Kate was the slightest bit self-conscious, she didn't let it show. After she'd emptied the kettle, she stood up and peeled the robe off to let it drop into a bundle at her feet. "Think there's any room in there for me?"

"I doubt it, but why don't you come a little closer?"

She did as she was told, taking a few steps toward him so Slocum could place a hand on her bare backside. He used that hand to guide her toward the tub until she was close enough for him to lean over and nip at her thigh.

"Oh, you're a wild one," she said. "I could tell that when you first signed that register. Let's see how wild you are." With that, she grabbed his hair and propped one foot up onto the side of the tub.

Slocum knew where he was being led and didn't mind it one bit. Not only did he allow Kate to pull his head between her legs, but he buried his tongue deep into her pussy the moment he got there.

"Even wilder than I thought," she gasped while tightening her grip on the back of his head.

Slocum reached up to grab her ass while flicking his tongue in and out of her. After only a few seconds of that, he pushed her leg off the side of the tub and stood up. Kate was putty in his hands and trembling so hard she couldn't stand up with him. He got out of the tub and moved around behind her. Kate twisted around to watch him, but was quickly turned back.

"Better hang on," Slocum said as he placed his hand on her back and pushed her forward. "You asked for wild, so that's what you're gonna get."

Kate couldn't lean forward fast enough. She gripped onto the edge of the tub with both hands and spread her legs just in time to accept his rigid length between them. Slocum could still taste her juices in his mouth, but the feel of her wrapped around his stiff pole was a whole lot sweeter. Kate's wide hips, trim waist, and swaying breasts made a fine hourglass shape, and her flesh was warm in his hands. When he grabbed her tight and drilled into her, Kate let out a deep-throated moan that filled the entire room.

"Damn, that's the way!" she cried. "Harder!"

Slocum pumped into her hard enough to slap against her backside. The impact made Kate squeal more, and when he pounded into her again, Slocum smacked the side of her ass hard enough to leave a red hand print.

Tossing her hair over her shoulder, Kate turned to look back at him. "Come on, now. You can fuck me harder than that."

Now it was Slocum's turn to smile. She started to tease him again, but couldn't say much of anything once he started pumping into her harder and harder. Kate arched her back while holding onto the tub. Soon, she was gripped by a powerful climax. Her hands may have left dents in the edge of the cheap metal tub when she bucked in time to his rhythm and shoved the whole thing several inches across the floor.

"Yes!" she screamed. "Keep at it!"

Slocum barely heard what she was saying. Her body felt too good to worry about something as inconsequential as words. Kate wriggled against him while letting her head hang down limply. When she looked back at him again, Slocum couldn't help noticing the flushed color of her cheeks and the enticing way she bit down on her thick lower lip.

"Come here," he said while pulling out of her and stepping back.

Kate stood up so Slocum could take her by the shoulders and make her face him. Excitement flashed in her eyes as she was pulled in close. Feeling his rigid manhood press against her body, she immediately reached down to stroke it with both hands.

He wanted to get back inside of her, but Kate had a different idea. She dropped to her knees and used both hands to guide him into her mouth. Her lips were just as soft as they looked, and Slocum didn't mind them being wrapped around him one bit. Placing his hands on either side of her head, he sifted through her hair as she sucked on him like a stick of candy.

It wouldn't take much to push him over the edge. That time was cut in half when she started sliding her tongue along the bottom of his shaft. Slocum closed his eyes and savored the wetness of her tongue. She finished him off and was still licking him when Slocum thought he heard movement outside the room.

"Are there many other rooms rented out?" he asked.

He could feel her smile more than see it. Kate stretched her arms up to run her hands flat against his stomach as she took him into her mouth once more.

The footsteps got closer, but Slocum wasn't of a mind to open the door. Since Kate was still unwilling to stop sucking him, he wasn't quick to step away from the bathtub. Suddenly, she moved away from him and jumped to her feet.

"In here, damn it!" she shouted.

The footsteps rushed toward the door and everything snapped into focus for Slocum. All of that yelling and carrying on from before hadn't been just her way of cutting loose. She'd been trying to draw the attention of whoever else was in the hotel. Slocum didn't need to see through walls to know that whoever was out there wasn't intending to shake hands and make nice.

When Slocum felt hands tugging at his arm, it was all he could do to keep from swinging at them. Kate clawed at him, fluttering her eyelids in a bad attempt to appear frightened.

"Don't open that door," she said. "Whoever is—"

"Don't give me that bullshit," Slocum growled. "You think I'm stupid? Get the fuck out of my way."

Naked and vulnerable, Kate moved aside so Slocum could get to the pile of clothes on the floor.

The first thing he found was his gun belt. Slocum took the Colt Navy from its holster and held onto it while he picked up his pants in one hand and did an awkward hopping dance to pull them on. He locked the door, but that wouldn't hold them for long.

"Who is it?" he asked while hastily buckling his belt. "Answer me, Kate. The moment you shouted for them to come here, you lost all your good graces with me, so you'd best answer real quick."

Kate slipped into her robe and lazily looped the belt around her waist to keep it mostly shut. "I don't know who he is, but I didn't have any choice in setting this up."

"You didn't, huh?"

"Too late to do anything about it now," she said with a shrug. "Too late for both of us."

Slocum knew plenty of ways to turn the tables on an overconfident bitch like her, but there simply wasn't enough time to indulge in anything like that. He picked up his gun, grabbed the door handle, and pulled the door open while jumping to one side. As he'd hoped, the men were taking a run at the door and were thrown off by the sudden removal of their obstacle.

One charged into the room and was tripped up by the bathtub. His shins hit the metal with a clang that was distorted by the water sloshing inside the large basin. Despite his best efforts to salvage his footing, he lost it and fell across the top of the tub. As much as Slocum would have liked to watch him kick and flail before hitting the floor, he had two other men to contend with. The second came in behind the first, skidding to a halt before following the first man over the tub. He was a large fellow with a bushy beard that sprouted from his face like a tangle of weeds. By the time he'd stopped, Slocum was rushing at him.

Even though he made a solid impact, Slocum simply didn't have enough momentum and bounced off of the larger man. He wasted no time before driving his left fist into the big man's gut. The uppercut sank in deep, driving a good portion of the wind from that man's lungs. Since there was a third man entering the room, Slocum hit the bearded fellow in the ribs with a chopping blow using the side of his Colt. Finely crafted iron did the job just as well as any club, weakening the bearded man enough for Slocum to shove him toward the bathtub, where he was quickly tripped up.

The third man wasn't wasting any time with punches. He raised a shotgun to aim at Slocum and was just about to pull his trigger when Slocum dropped to one knee and fired from the hip. His Colt barked once, spitting a piece of lead that Slocum knew wouldn't hit its mark. His aim was better than he'd anticipated, thanks mostly to the fact that he was only a few paces away from his target. A shredded piece of the shotgunner's shirt flew off, accompanied by a spray of blood as if he'd been slashed by an invisible claw. His face twisted into a pained grimace and he staggered back into the hall to reload.

A surprised yelp echoed through the room as the bearded man lost his struggle to keep from falling over. After being pushed into the tub, he'd somehow caught himself with one hand against the side, which left him in a precarious balance. Thanks to all the splashing that had come before, the edge was slippery and he lost his grip. He slipped, hit the side of the tub on one arm, and flopped into the water.

"All right, big man," Slocum growled as he circled around

the tub so it was between him and the door. "Tell me why you're here and be quick about it."

Possibly drawing strength from the fact that his partners were still in the fight, the bearded man spat the water from his mouth and gripped the tub so he could haul himself up.

Grabbing onto the bearded man's thick mane of hair with his free hand, Slocum held him in place while knocking the first man back to the floor with a well-placed boot. That one was still dazed after his less-than-graceful entrance and had been hanging onto the side of the tub. When Slocum's boot pounded against his ribs, he cursed, dropped to the floor, and curled into a defensive ball.

Firing a shot into the hallway to keep the shotgunner in check, Slocum pushed the bearded man's head beneath the water. "Tell me!" he bellowed.

Although the shotgunner had been momentarily distracted by the lead coming his way, the weapon in his hands gave him the courage to make a stand. The scattergun roared and sent a storm of lead into the hotel room. Fortunately, Slocum had caught sight of the man in the hallway a split second before the firestorm headed his way. He dropped to the floor as buckshot ripped through the bathtub and a few stray pieces of lead grazed his back.

Instead of sticking his head up to present the shotgunner with a good target, Slocum crawled around the tub and fired two quick shots at the doorway. The first one caught the shotgunner's attention, and the second caught him square in the chest. When the man in the hallway dropped, his finger tensed around his trigger, and he sent his second barrel straight into the ceiling.

The barrel of the Colt Navy was still smoking when Slocum pressed it against the face of the first man to storm his room. "Start tellin' me what I want to know!"

The man didn't need any more prompting than that. Even if he didn't know what was on Slocum's mind, he would have gotten to it eventually as the words started flowing from his mouth. "Harper sent us in here to flush you out! He tracked you here and paid us to come and kill you!"

"Flush me out or kill me? Make up your damn mind."

"Either one! It didn't matter! We were just supposed to get you out of this room one way or the other! We're through, though. Just let us go and we're done!"

"You're right you're done," Slocum replied.

"No! I mean—"

Slocum ended the other man's babbling with a straight punch to the nose. Shifting his aim to the man in the tub, he asked, "What about you, big man?"

But that one wasn't talking. His head lay on the side of the tub and one arm flopped over the edge along with one of his legs. His eyes were open, but there wasn't any life in them. The first shotgun blast had seen to that. Slocum nudged him just to be certain, but all that did was send ripples through the crimson-stained water inside the tub.

"Looks like you're the last one standing," Slocum said to the man with the broken nose, who'd started crawling away in a pathetic attempt to escape.

Sensing he'd been spotted, the man barely seemed to notice the guns lying on the floor, which had been dropped by himself and his partner in the tub. His hands were trembling too hard to pick anything up anyhow as he desperately tried to crawl around the other end of the tub. When he felt Slocum grab him by the collar, he frantically scraped at the floor and sputtered for mercy.

"You," Slocum growled. "Come out from back there."

"I'm right here," the man on the floor gasped. "I'm done. I told you already, just let me go!"

"Not you," Slocum said as he slammed the gunman's head against the side of the tub. "Her."

All that could be seen of Kate was the top few strands of her hair poking up from behind the bed. Having been called out directly, she poked her head up from the spot she'd found between the wall and the bed. Her face was white as the sheets and her eyes nervously darted toward the window looking down onto the street.

Waving toward the two dead gunmen and the unconscious one propped against the tub, Slocum asked, "Are these the men who arranged this?"

She shook her head. "It was a fella in fancy clothes with brown hair. He had a big nose and one of those hats that . . ." Too nervous to come up with the proper word, she began tracing the shape of a bowler hat on top of her head.

"And what did he say to you?"

"He paid me to make sure this hotel was cleared out except for you, me, and them. He also wanted me to try and get you alone without your gun. I thought I might be able to knock you out while you were in the bath. But," she added with a wicked smile, "you distracted me."

Not feeling the slightest effect from the look she was giving him, Slocum said, "That means he's nearby. Take me to him."

"I swear I don't know where to find him."

Slocum raised his Colt with a sharp motion that made Kate jump back against the wall. He opened the cylinder and went through the practiced motions of removing the spent rounds so he could reload. "I've been through enough bullshit for one night. You gave me one hell of a bath, but it wasn't good enough to make up for the rest. Tell me where to find that fancy-britches with the round hat." Snapping the cylinder shut and keeping the gun in hand, he added, "Or I may lose my patience."

"He should have been here by now. He . . . he wanted to catch you personally. He told me so when he was paying me. It was real important."

"I bet it was."

Something thumped within another room. The sound caused her to jump as if it was a gunshot, and when the sound of a slamming door could be heard, Kate backed into her hiding spot as if she meant to push all the way through the wall.

"Is that him?" Slocum asked.

"We're the only ones in the hotel," she said quickly. "Just don't let him near me. Please, I swore I'd do my part and he'll be mad if he sees this. He's crazy!"

No matter what Slocum may have thought of her, he didn't like seeing any woman as frightened as she was at that moment. Fear was written on her face as clearly as if it had been scratched there by a rusty nail.

"How many more are there?" Slocum asked. Since his question hadn't caught her ear, he leaned down closer to her and slapped the bed to shake her from whatever thoughts were rolling through her head. "Answer me, Kate. How many more are in here?"

"Just the one with the fancy clothes and maybe one more."

"You sure about that?"

She shook her head violently and huddled against the wall.

Knowing he wasn't going to get any more out of her, Slocum snatched his shirt from the floor and pulled it on to fight the chill from the wind that shook the glass panes in the window frames. He collected the other guns strewn on the floor, dropping one into the bathwater and keeping the other for himself. Slocum stepped into the hallway, which immediately triggered an explosion of gunfire from the far end.

Lead punched into the wall and through the door frame, and hissed toward the stairs with no sign of letting up. When Slocum fell back into the room, he had to take a moment to make sure he was still in one piece. Although the gouges the buckshot had ripped along his back were still aching, he seemed to have all his other parts. As he waited for the shots to stop, he checked to count three rounds left in the cylinder of the gun he'd picked up.

As soon as the thunder stopped, Slocum leaned toward the door and shouted into the hallway, "That all you can do, Mike? Shoot at anything that moves?"

A door at the other end of the hall slammed shut and muffled footsteps rattled in the distance.

"Is there another way out of here from this floor, Kate?"

"Not unless he jumps out the window."

Slocum glanced over to his own window, which was definitely large enough for a man to step through, and looked out onto the street. "Is there anything for him to climb on?"

She nodded. "He wanted the room above the front awning. Paid special for it."

"Shit."

No matter how prudent it would have been to bide his time and wait for a better chance to go after the bounty hunter, Slocum could already hear sounds from the other end of the nearly empty hotel that could easily be a window rattling in its frame and a man hopping out onto the awning. A few more seconds and Harper would be sliding to the street, where he surely had an escape route plotted out. If weasels like him were good for anything, it was planning an escape.

"Not if I can help it," Slocum snarled under his breath.

Holding both guns at the ready, Slocum charged out of the room, kept his back to one wall, and rushed down the hall. The fact that he hadn't been able to pull on his boots worked to his advantage because it kept his steps from thumping the way the others were throughout the hotel. Even so, the floor was creaking enough to make him certain that Harper knew he was coming.

Thanks to the scraping of feet against the awning and the last few rattles of the window, Slocum was able to pinpoint which room Harper was in. Keeping as low as possible, he set his sights on that door and made his approach. He tucked the borrowed gun under his arm so he could reach out to grab the door handle. As soon as he gave it a try, a shot blasted through the wooden barrier no more than eight inches over his head.

Swearing loudly, Slocum leapt to one side as more shots punched through the door. Kate had actually tried to help him on that score. She'd warned him that there might be two men left instead of just one. That meant one to make plenty of noise while climbing out through the window and another to spring the trap once Slocum came running. The fact that he'd played into that trap so well was Slocum's damn fault.

So he'd been baited by a particular sound. There was no reason why he couldn't use that same trick himself.

"Damn!" he grunted while throwing himself back against the lower portion of the wall. Even as his back hit and his body slid to the floor, Slocum watched the door that had just been blown to pieces. His senses were sharp enough to spot every splinter from each bullet hole and, more importantly, hear the sounds of the man on the other side of the door reloading his gun.

Slocum approached the door, stood to one side, and used one heel to knock it open. When no shots came, he jumped into the doorway while holding both guns in front of him. Although that wasn't a practical way to fire the weapons, it made one hell of an imposing picture. At least the man standing just inside the room seemed to think so.

He was a lean fellow in his late twenties with a round face and a thin mustache. The style of his clothes was the same as Michael Harper's: fancy yet rumpled. Caught after having replaced a few of his rounds, he snapped the cylinder shut.

"Not another move," Slocum warned.

Behind the young gunman, the window was wide open. The scraping of boots against the awning was soon followed by a huffing breath and the impact of something heavy against the street.

When Slocum started walking toward the window, his

path was blocked by the other man. Extending both arms to point the guns at him, Slocum said, "Drop your gun and step aside."

The other man held his ground.

"Whatever Harper's paying you ain't enough to die for. Don't be a fool. You already lost this one. Drop the gun and step aside."

"You're a killer and a coward," the man said. "This is a chance for you to come along to take what's coming to you. After this, it gets ugly."

Slocum could hear footsteps crunching on the street below. They were fading fast and would soon be too far gone for him to follow. "This is as ugly as it needs to get for you," he said. "I don't know who you are and I don't give a damn. Harper's the one I want."

The other man shook his head. "You're a back-shooting son of a bitch. I ain't afraid of you." To prove his point, the young man brought his gun up to fire a shot at Slocum. He almost got a chance to squeeze his trigger before Slocum burned him down with a single shot from each of the guns he carried. Both rounds hit, but the one from the Colt Navy was the one that did him in. The gunman fell over, his last twitch sending a round through the floor.

When Slocum finally got to the window, all he could see was an empty street.

12

Slocum's blood was flowing so quickly through his veins that he felt capable of running all the way back to Chicago if that meant getting his hands wrapped around Harper's neck. But Harper wasn't the root of his problem, and running off half-cocked was a real good way to catch a bullet between the eyes. The dandy bounty hunter may have skinned out of the hotel, but he did leave a lot of bags behind. Slocum used the fire in his belly to help him tear through those bags in short order.

A light footstep brushed against the floor in the hall, causing Slocum to turn toward it with his Colt held at the ready. Kate stood there with her hands pressed to her face and her eyes wide as saucers.

"Another one?" she gasped while staring at the dead man.

"Yeah," Slocum said while dumping the contents of the last bag onto the bed. "That's what happens in an ambush. Did you expect we'd all be slapping each other on the back and eating cake?"

"No, but I . . . I . . ."

"How much did he pay you for this?"

"A hundred dollars."

Slocum raised his eyebrows while sifting through Harper's things. "That's a lot of money. Did he part with it easily?"

"He was specific in what he wanted, but he paid me sure enough."

So the bounty hunter didn't spend all of his cash on clothes. That meant he had funds of his own or someone backing him. Neither one of those options struck Slocum as very good.

"Do you . . . want some of that money?" Kate asked.

Before he could take her up on that offer, Slocum found something even better. It was a newspaper that had been stuffed into the bottom of the bag to be used as a lining. Despite the paper having soaked up a good amount of water from the rain or whatever other conditions that bag had been dragged through, there was still enough print visible for him to make out the top section of the front page.

"Keep your money," Slocum told her, "but you'll do something to make up for selling me out."

"Anything. I'll go wherever you want and do whatever you want . . . again."

"That's not the sort of thing I'm talking about. If anyone asks what happened here, you can tell them whatever the hell you want in regards to why the shots were fired. Whatever story you come up with, just make sure it ends with me being killed. You understand?"

"I think so. Why would you want me to—"

Slocum wheeled around and came at her with all the rage that had been boiling inside of him. One way or another, those rumors were coming to an end. "The why don't matter. You'll pick a corpse and tell folks it's John Slocum. If I don't hear rumors of my own demise soon enough, I'll come back to give this town one more corpse to gossip about. You understand now?"

She couldn't nod fast enough. "Which one should I say was you?"

After scooping as much of Harper's belongings that he could fit into one bag, Slocum headed for the door. "I don't care," he said while walking down the hall to get his boots and the rest of his clothes. "Just so long as it ain't the ugliest of the bunch."

The rooms above the Creek House Saloon made the one Slocum had rented look like royal living quarters in comparison. Then again, the hallway wasn't shot to hell and there weren't bodies on the floor. After receiving enough of a pounding to shake the door on its hinges, it was pulled open just far enough for one suspicious eye and the barrel of a gun to poke out. Both of them belonged to Daniel Sykes.

"Come to ask for my help already?" Sykes asked as he pulled the door open the rest of the way.

Slocum stormed into a room that was too small for him to take two full strides without hitting a wall and too cramped for him to stand upright without knocking his head against the slanted ceiling. "Remember that bounty hunter I was talking about?"

"The dandy with the bowler?"

"That's the one. He paid me a visit."

By this time, Sykes had picked out the blood soaking through the back of Slocum's shirt as well as the scent of burned gunpowder that was in his clothes. Sykes was chuckling as he checked the hallway and shut the door. "Do we need to worry about him anymore?"

"Yeah. The slippery little prick jumped out a window and was gone before I could catch up to him."

"Well then, let's get after him! He can't have gotten far and I know a few places where he might be holed up."

Slocum threw Harper's bag at him so it hit Sykes flat against his chest, stopping the man before he opened the door again. "Take a look in there and tell me if you find anything important."

"Unless that bounty hunter's in here, I don't give a shit."

"If you know some places where Harper may be, we can pay them a visit. Otherwise, I don't want to waste any more time on that asshole."

"Waste time?" Sykes asked. "The son of a bitch came after both of us, and you think getting to him is a waste of time?"

"Harper's not the real problem. Take a look inside that bag."

Gritting his teeth, Sykes stomped over to the rickety bed and dumped the contents of the bag onto its lumpy surface. Although he'd been impatient and flustered with Slocum's request, he quickly saw the reasoning behind it as several water-stained and dog-eared copies of cheaply bound books fell from the bag. "What the hell is this?"

"A whole library of bullshit," Slocum replied. "I only sifted through a few of them, but none of it's very complimentary to either of us."

"And not just us," Sykes said as he leafed through one book entitled *Last Stand in Louisiana*. "This mentions an associate of mine. I've never even seen this one before."

"If Harper is reading and believing this stuff, that's one problem. If he's just the first one to come after us, that's a whole other set of complications. From what Ian told me, there's gonna be plenty more of these books on the way, and after that happens there may be other bounty hunters out there who get it in their heads to come after us. The stories will take a life of their own and it'll be a tough fire to stamp out."

Sykes gripped a book in both hands and clenched fists around it. The flimsy pages crumpled easily before he finally ripped the thing in two. "I got enough to worry about in regards to things I done. The last thing I need is some asshole writer adding more to that list."

"Which brings me to the reason I came over here. We need to get to the root of this problem."

"You're damn right we do." Snatching another book from the pile, Sykes held it in a trembling hand as if that bunch of yellowed paper was the bane of his existence. "We gotta find this writer." Turning the book so he could get a look at the name on the cover, he snarled, "Edward Corrington. I told you this much already, so now you're finally with me?"

"Yeah. I'm with you."

"Good. 'Cause when I get my hands on this asshole, I'm gonna—"

Slocum cut him short by forcing him to loosen his grip on the book. Taking it away from him the way he would cautiously remove a bone from a hungry dog's mouth, he said, "Most of these books are kindling as far as I'm concerned, but I want this one."

"Why?"

"Because I'm not sure where to find Edward Corrington. What about you?"

Scowling at the book as if trying to live up to his end of the hungry dog comparison, Sykes replied, "If he ain't gonna show up to talk to this printer, then no. But that bounty hunter may know, and the longer we dawdle here, the more of a chance we're giving that asshole of slipping away again."

"And if all else fails," Slocum said while opening the book to the first page and showing it to him, "we know the next stop we need to make."

On the first page of *Last Stand in Louisiana*, there was an inscription that read, "To Michael, best regards. E. Corrington—Sept. 9 St. Louis, Missouri."

A smile slid onto Sykes's face that was about as friendly as a hiss from a rattlesnake.

The places on Sykes's list were a hotel on the other side of town and the saloon next to the one where he'd rented his room. The saloon was full of people, but none of them was the one they were after. On the way to the hotel, Slocum spotted a group of lawmen carrying shotguns and walking with purpose in the opposite direction. He kept his head down and stayed out of the lawmen's way. Fortunately, Sykes didn't need to be told to do the same.

"Think them boys are looking in on our bounty hunter friend?" Sykes asked.

Slocum cast one glance at the lawmen's backs and kept walking. "More likely they're checking in on all the shots that were fired. If so, they're gonna find some of Harper's partners. Might be best if we're not in town when they do."

"I think I'm gonna like workin' with you just fine."

13

"I assure you, sir, you do not want to test me, so I will only ask you once more. Where is John Slocum?"

Terrance was taking a turn behind the bar when Harper had stormed into his theater. It was the start of the dinner show and the girls were kicking their heels up while accompanied by a bawdy tune. The customers who weren't enthralled by that sight were wrapped up in their own games. The roulette wheel was spinning, but this time the man behind it was a longtime friend of Terrance's. All was well in the Stamper. At least, it was until Harper pointed a gun at the theater's owner.

"I'll tell you the same thing I told you before," Terrance said dryly. "After he left here, I don't know where he went."

"You paid him to kill Bo. You're a friend of his, aren't you?"

"I'd like to think so, but I ain't his keeper. Even if I did know where he was, why the hell would I tell you?"

112

Harper's youthful face twisted into an angry scowl. He looked down as if to make sure the gun was still in his hand.

"Maybe you should look behind you," Terrance said.

Risking only a quick glance back, Harper spotted the two armed men who'd taken positions behind him. Holstering the .32 in a small holster under his arm, Harper said, "I don't think you know Slocum as well as you think you do."

"I don't?"

"He's a cold-blooded killer and a murderer of innocents."

"Sounds just terrible," Terrance sighed. "I'll weep over it once you're out of here. Now you can leave through the door or the window. Take a second to think it over."

Anyone who'd seen Terrance before Slocum had arrived could see a big difference in the way the theater owner carried himself. After ridding his place of the bad element and putting Bo into the ground, he was bolder and more confident. He'd also hired new men to protect his interests. The ones Harper saw when he turned around weren't familiar to him. But, familiar or not, they carried sawed-off shotguns partially covered by long coats so as not to rile up the customers. If Slocum was there, he would have shown himself. And if Terrance was inclined to help Harper in finding him, he would have shown a sign of buckling by now. Empty-handed after his ride from Braverly, Harper walked past the men with the shotguns and left the Stamper for good.

As soon as the doors were shut behind him and the music faded to a muffled wail, Harper stuffed his hands into his pockets and balled them into fists. He'd wanted to pull his trigger when he was back there, but that wouldn't have been proper. He'd wanted to drag Terrance outside and show him the dirt that was stained by blood that had flowed through Bo's veins. For all of his posturing, Terrance Pinder wasn't anything more than a killer himself. Perhaps he could be reminded of that fact if Harper decided to pay him a visit once the theater's gunmen weren't itching for a fight.

Harper nodded and let out a calming breath. "For everything, there is a time."

As if in response to those words, two men made themselves known by stepping out of the shadows across the street. They were killers as well, but unlike the theater owner, James and Cam didn't care who knew it. In some respects, that made them easier for the bounty hunter to tolerate.

James waved impatiently at him even after Harper crossed the street and approached him. When they were standing face-to-face, James said, "You're that dandy that was after Slocum."

"What business is that of yours?"

"We know where he went."

"Why should I believe you?"

"He's at a little town south of here," Cam said in a rush. "Braverly's the name of the place."

"I already came from there," Harper said dismissively. "You don't have anything else I need?"

"We know what he's after," James said.

"And when did he tell you all of this?" Harper scoffed. "Did the three of you sit down to sip tea and swap stories?"

James stepped up until he was close enough to knock the other man back with his chest. "No, smart-ass. We got a friend who still works for the shithead who runs that theater. How do you think we managed to get my girls in there so easy in the first place?"

Harper didn't know the details of the other two men's history with the Stamper, and he didn't care to learn it. He did, however, have a good grip on knowing when someone was feeding him a line of manure. James struck Harper as too anxious to be an effective liar and too ignorant to try and play him like a fiddle.

As if sensing the change in Harper's attitude, James said, "Slocum's after some writer who put him in a book or something."

"Yeah?"

"That's right. He went down to Braverly to try and catch up with him. If he ain't there, we should be able to find someone who saw what happened once Slocum got his hands on that writer fella."

"The writer wasn't in Braverly," Harper replied. "But I can find out where he'll be."

"All right, then," Cam said in a nervous voice. "If Slocum could have found out the same thing, then we know where he'll be too. That puts us right where we started, which is a prime spot to head him off and bring him down."

"You came after him once already," James said. "Seein' as how he made you look like a fool that time, I'd bet you want to see him dead just as much as we do. I just heard that there's a price on his head."

"That's right. But I've tracked him this far. I can do the rest on my own."

Nodding toward the spot where Slocum had been when Bo was gunned down, James said, "Funny, but I seem to recall you not having much luck when you took him on by yourself."

"That was unfortunate timing is all."

"Yeah, real unfortunate for you to walk straight up to a known gunhand like Slocum while our partner is getting cut in half in the street. If you'd had Slocum's undivided attention, it would've been you dead in the dirt instead of Bo. Look me in the eyes and tell me I'm wrong."

Harper did look James in the eyes, but he couldn't dispute the other man's claim. In fact, as he thought back to how things had gone that day, as well as the night in Braverly, he realized that James had more of a point than he could possibly know. It also seemed as if he might know a thing or two that could be useful. "So you've heard of Slocum?"

"Yeah. He's taken on his share of bad men and lived to tell the tale. I spoke to some folks who come up here from New Mexico, and they say he's done some damage there as well. There's supposed to be a price on his head in regards to some old business, but you'd probably know more about that."

Harper nodded sagely, even though he hadn't bothered looking into those older reward notices.

"I bet we could find him even quicker if we did it together instead of apart," James continued. "Some of my girls have scattered since that whole scuffle, and the rest are a little skittish, so they could use the time to rest up. Me and Cam will be going after Slocum anyways, so there's no reason the three of us should be steppin' on each other's toes."

Cam's face was hard to read, simply because it didn't stay still for very long. For the most part, he was content to watch the street and twitch at every sound that came from the Stamper. Considering the show that was being put on in there, that was a whole lot of twitching. Still, there was a spark in that one's eyes that Harper thought he could use. At the very least, the fidgeting young man would make excellent bait.

"So you want to work for me?" Harper asked.

"With you is more like it," James snapped. "But yeah. We all got a bone to pick with Slocum."

"What do you want for payment?"

"He's got a price on his head, right?"

Harper nodded.

"Well you can keep that," James said. "Cashing in something like that would just involve talkin' to a bunch of law dogs, and I'd rather not have any part of that. All I want is his head."

Raising an eyebrow, Harper asked, "You want to take his head?"

"Well not on a pike or nothin', but I want his blood on my hands. I wanna be known as the one to kill him since that'll be how it pans out anyways. And when the stories start to fly, I want you to back 'em up. Every little bit helps."

James puffed out his chest and shifted his attention to the theater. "I'm comin' back to this town as more than I am right now." Shooting a quick glance to his partner, he added, "I mean both Cam and me of course."

Harper took notice of the uneasiness in Cam's face and replied, "Of course."

"I can't abide bein' run out of any place," James continued. "If I come back as the man who killed the best gunman Terrance Pinder could afford, I'll have the run of that theater. And once I get the run of one place, running the next ones will be that much easier."

"Sounds like a good plan," Harper said. "How soon can you start?"

14

When they reached St. Louis, it didn't take Slocum and his new partner long to track down where Edward Corrington had been. The writer had dropped off a shipment of his books at several general stores and stayed around to sign copies for whoever bought them on the first day. After that, he'd headed south along the Mississippi River for some event that none of the store owners knew much about. Once that same story had been confirmed by at least half a dozen others, Slocum took it at face value. From there, the route seemed fairly cut-and-dried. Well, maybe not particularly dry.

Slocum leaned against the rail on the upper deck of the steamboat paddling its way down the river. Although he normally preferred to ride at his own pace, there were benefits to this method of travel. Not the least of which was the refreshing spray of mist against his face on a sunny day. After all that had happened recently, it did him some good to let his shoulders ease down from up around his ears.

There were only a few other passengers on board, along with several horses. The boat itself had seen better days, and nearly every plank in her was warped to some degree.

When Sykes came up the steps leading from the main cabin, he nearly pulled the rail from the wall after stumbling on the weathered boards. "Damn thing's probably gonna sink before its next stop," he grumbled.

"If it does, then our problems won't seem so bad," Slocum offered.

"Sure. We'll swim to shore, dry off, and get shot at by some other bunch of addle-brained gunmen who read too many of those yellowback books."

"So did you find out anything useful or did you just stagger around bellyaching to the crew?"

Sykes stood beside him, gripped the rail as if his life depended on it, and then spewed a portion of his last meal into the river. After spitting the last of it out, he wiped his mouth with his sleeve and sighed. "That's better." When he spoke again, it was with renewed vigor. "The fellow tending to the horses belowdecks remembers our man Corrington well enough. He says that writer was fussier than a princess when it came to his horse. All I had to do was mention the fits Corrington threw and that jostled memories from the rest of the crew as well."

"What sort of memories?"

"Like all the yarns he was spinning during his ride up this same river into St. Louis."

"Did they take him back downriver?" Slocum asked.

"Oh yeah. Corrington paid extra for the captain to wait for him so he wouldn't have to break in another crew. He drove them crazy all over again when he wouldn't shut his damn mouth about all sorts of bullshit nobody wanted to hear."

"I know how they feel," Slocum grunted.

Sykes continued on despite Slocum's sarcasm. "And because of all this, they all remembered where they left him off because they were finally rid of the son of a bitch."

Until now, Slocum had been prepared to ride the river south to the next largest port. It made the most sense considering all of the places that the writer had stopped along the waterway. If he didn't figure something out in the meantime, Slocum had figured on looking for the next link in the chain at a place that sold the books. What he hadn't counted on was Sykes actually stepping up and doing something useful.

Still wary of the other man's detective skills, Slocum asked, "You got a notion of where he went?"

"Better than a notion. All the crew says they dumped him off a few miles downriver, where he was supposed to catch a stage into Perryville."

"Perryville, huh? Are they sure about that part?"

Sykes nodded enthusiastically. "That writer didn't shut up about it. Kept spouting off about dropping his new book off there. Invited everyone to come buy it and wouldn't take no for an answer. The captain of this heap couldn't get the hell away from that dock fast enough. He even sounded cautious about going back. Probably worried that writer might catch a whiff of him and try gnawing his ear off with some more of his goddamn stories."

Holding onto the rail, Slocum looked toward the bow as if he could see far enough past the front of the boat to get a look at where they were headed. In the time he and Sykes had been traveling together, Slocum hadn't met up with any more bounty hunters. Then again, he'd been doing his best to keep from meeting anyone at all until his temper had had a chance to simmer down. The folks in St. Louis had been friendly enough, but none of them had been told Slocum or Sykes's real name. And the moment he'd heard that Corrington wasn't in town any longer, Slocum was on his way out.

"So how much farther is it to port?" Slocum asked.

"We should be there before supper."

"Think we could convince the captain to stop there one more time?"

Sykes beamed proudly and slapped him on the back. "Already made the arrangements."

* * *

If Slocum had had any doubt about Sykes's story, they were put to rest by the crew themselves when they tied off at the short pier sticking out into the river from a crooked shoreline near Perryville. The horses were saddled and led to the top of the gangplank before the boat had come to a full stop. They were led to shore at the same time Slocum and Sykes were all but pushed overboard. Even though he was paid in full, the captain wasn't anxious for repeat business.

"You ain't bringing that writer back, are you?" the stout bald man asked.

Slocum didn't have to do one bit of acting when he replied, "If I have it my way, you won't hear from that writer again for a good long time."

That seemed to please the boat captain just fine, and he sealed the deal by shaking Slocum's hand. "I go up and down this river all the time. If you two need a ride back, just wait for me here and I'll be along. So long as I don't see that writer with ya, I'll toss you a line."

"Sounds good."

And before they could get their land legs back, the two of them were leading their horses by the reins as the steamboat chugged away.

"Good thing we didn't have much by way of baggage," Sykes huffed, "or it would've been tossed into the trees."

"Seems our Mr. Corrington has that effect on folks."

"Yep. I suppose he does."

It was just under ten miles to Perryville from the spot where they'd been dumped onto the riverbank. Slocum and Sykes led their horses to the trail that led into town, climbed into their saddles, and tapped their heels against their animals' sides. The horses were a bit unsteady at first, but they were also anxious to get moving after being cooped up in the stalls below the boat's deck.

Slocum found he had the same problem as the tan horse

beneath him. The biggest difference being that he wasn't able to stretch his legs while getting his bearings. He'd simply traded the slow, back-and-forth rocking of the boat for the horse's faster front-to-back rocking. Before too long, his innards felt as if they were being tossed around like a handful of dice. Midway through their ride, he insisted on watering the horses even though the animals were willing to run for another mile. He thought he might vomit worse than Sykes had done while on the boat, but somehow he managed to keep it down. A few splashes of water on his face got him feeling good enough to ride the rest of the way into town, but by the time he got to Perryville, Slocum was more than a little green around the gills.

Grinning victoriously as he climbed down from his saddle, Sykes looked over at him and asked, "You gonna be all right, John? I'd swear you were gettin' seasick."

"I'm fine," Slocum snapped.

"How about we get something to eat? I'm starving. What do you say to a nice, juicy steak? I like mine with plenty of fat around the edges to get all crispy on a fire. That just melts in your mouth like a sloppy spoonful of butter."

"Will you shut your damn mouth?"

"You sure you ain't sick?" Sykes chided him, obviously knowing the answer to his own question.

Once he was down from his saddle, Slocum pulled in a breath and felt his boots press down into the comforting, unmoving earth. He placed his hands on his hips, let out the air he'd gulped down, and returned Sykes's gaze. "I'm sick of hearing you squawk. Does that count?"

"A man's got to make certain his partner's in prime working condition, that's all. We may just cross our man's path at any moment."

"Or we may have to find another path to catch up to the bastard. I'm starting to wonder if this asshole isn't just some sort of ghost."

The smile on Sykes's face turned cold at first and then

fell off of him completely. His eyes narrowed into slits and he nodded toward one of the nearby buildings. "Then it looks like this whole town believes in spooks."

Slocum looked at what had caught Sykes's eye and found a door to a general store completely covered in very familiar notices. There were several that overlapped, but he immediately recognized the picture on one of the sheets of paper as the scene from *Six-Gun Devil*. The rest were from other books attributed to Edward Corrington, and the closer he got to them, the sicker Slocum felt.

He knocked the door open with the palm of his hand, grabbed hold of a notice, and ripped it off in one angry motion. Once inside, Slocum stalked over to the counter, where an old woman sat beside a rusty cash register. She had a terrified look on her face and a set of knitting needles in her gnarled hands. Before Slocum could say a word, Sykes rushed past him.

"Excuse me, ma'am," Sykes said breathlessly. "We just got into town. Is it true a writer came through here not too long ago?"

The old woman scooted to the edge of her stool, set herself down, and placed her knitting carefully on the counter. Glaring up at Slocum without a bit of fear, she scolded them. "He's still here. You two would have seen as much for yourself if you would've read what was on that paper instead of ripping it down."

"Where is he?" Slocum asked.

"You ever hear you can catch more flies with honey than vinegar?"

"I certainly have, ma'am," Sykes replied. "My partner's just a little under the weather after a long ride and a longer float down the river."

The old woman's stern expression softened just a bit when she heard that. "I don't take to the water myself. I say if the good Lord wanted us to travel that way, he would've webbed our toes."

Sykes nudged Slocum a little too hard to be friendly, but just about right to shove him away from the counter.

Swallowing his first impulse to shove Sykes into a pile of blankets, Slocum turned away from the counter and walked down the first of the store's two aisles.

"My apologies about the advertisements on your door," Sykes continued. "We come a long way to be here. All the way from St. Louis on that damned boat. Pardon my language."

She finally relaxed and waved at him as if shooing a gnat. "I've heard worse from my Frank. Especially when we used to go to St. Louis to visit his family. I thought that damn boat would be the death of me."

"And a stagecoach ain't much better, is it?"

Her eyes widened as if Sykes had just peered into her soul. "It true, isn't it? With all that shaking and swaying, a person's bound to rattle their stomach up through their nose." Picking up her knitting, she settled into her original rhythm.

"So you say the writer of them books is here in Perryville?" Sykes asked.

"Sure is. He was supposed to go to St. Louis as well, but he wasn't gone long. I don't know if he even made the trip."

"Would you know where we could find him? My partner and I are admirers of his work."

"Like I said before, read the sign."

"Sorry, ma'am. I never was much of one for schoolin'."

With that, Sykes completely turned the tables on the old woman. He'd already gotten her to ease up, but now she looked as if she'd been the one overstepping her bounds. "Oh my goodness, I'm sorry about that. I must sound just awful talking down to you that way." Suddenly, her brow furrowed and she asked, "If you can't read, then how is it you're so familiar with Mr. Corrington's works?"

"My partner's the smart one," Sykes replied. "He reads them front to back and then tells me all about it. Makes for a whole lot of talking, but a long ride passes well enough."

Apparently that was good enough for her, because the old woman smiled warmly and nodded. "Just like how I used to read to my Frank. Isn't that sweet?"

Slocum approached the counter again. As before, his hands were full with paper, but it wasn't the kind that had been tacked to a door. Instead, it had been folded into several books. Each of the volumes bore one of the wildly dramatic drawings that had become familiar trademarks of Corrington's rubbish. "Yeah," he said under his breath. "Real sweet. I haven't seen these before. How much for the lot?"

Despite his unfriendly entrance and their shaky introduction, the old woman looked at Slocum now as if she would kiss him from across the counter and invite him to stay for supper. "Hand them over and I'll figure it up."

"And what about that pocketknife there, ma'am?" Sykes inquired. "The one in the glass case?"

The woman set the books into a neat pile on the counter and shuffled merrily to the case adjacent to the cash register.

"Aren't you going a little overboard with your spending?" Slocum asked.

"*Our* spending," Sykes corrected. "I'll have to borrow some of that money you got in Chicago."

"Forget it."

"Aww, look how happy she is. Doesn't it do your heart good to see that smile?"

The old woman was smiling all right. Her smile became even wider when she was finished adding up the total of Slocum's purchase and poking the keys of her register.

Considering there was still plenty more the woman could tell them if she was of a mind to, Slocum kept her spirits up by paying his bill in full. The sting from handing over the money was soothed when she started talking about all of the visits she'd had from the delightful and prolific Edward Corrington.

15

Slocum's cash reserves took another hit when it came time to rent a room. The Ole Miss Wheelhouse was a fine hotel, but their prices were outrageous considering both beds were only slightly larger than cots. He would have spread out his bedroll in the same stall as his horse if not for the fact that the old woman at the store swore that was the hotel favored by the town's literary visitor. Sure enough, Slocum spotted the writer's flowing signature on the register when he signed it.

"Just the one room for both of you?" the spindly fellow behind the front desk asked.

"Yeah," Sykes grunted. "Just the one room," he added bitterly.

"You want your own room?" Slocum asked. "You can pay for it."

"Maybe I should find another hotel. You know, to make sure we're spread out to cover the whole town."

Slocum shrugged. "Fine. If I happen to be the first one to find what we're after, I can take care of things as I see fit."

Like any outlaw, Sykes thought along twisted lines. Even though Slocum left out a whole lot in that roundabout promise, Sykes quickly arrived at an interpretation that brought a scowl to his face. "I'll have my own room, thank you very much."

"I know you tend to wander," Slocum said. "Maybe you should stay close so I can keep an eye on you."

"My cousin Gary had a problem like that," the man behind the desk said with a thick Virginian accent. "He was always a bit slow, but got downright tricky after he took a kick to the head from his favorite pony. Ma had to feed him and everything."

Slocum couldn't keep from laughing, but managed to get his hand up to cover his mouth and pass it off as clearing his throat.

The act wasn't fooling Sykes, however. "I ain't slow."

"That's what Gary always used to say," the clerk replied with a condescending nod.

That was too much for Slocum, who had to launch into a full coughing fit to hide his laughter.

"Your room's at the top of the stairs, second on the left," the clerk announced before anyone else had a chance to speak. He handed the key to Slocum and asked, "You want any help with your bags?"

"Not at all." Kicking the pair of saddlebags they'd brought in, Slocum looked at Sykes and said, "Be a good boy and carry these up to the room, will you?"

Sykes turned his back on both of them and stalked toward the staircase. "Go fuck yourself."

When Slocum raised his eyebrows at that, the clerk nodded again. "Gary had a problem with foul language too."

Hefting both sets of saddlebags onto his shoulders, Slocum said, "Maybe this one needs a good kick to the head."

The clerk shrugged and went back to his paperwork.

Sykes's footsteps were heavy enough for them to be heard throughout the place. When he got to the second floor,

Slocum only needed to look for the door that was still swinging on its hinges to find their room. Strolling in and dropping his bags on the floor, he said, "That fellow behind the desk was already worth the high price of this place."

"What the hell do we need one room for?" Sykes growled. "You wanna get close to me, John? Is that it?"

"Watch your mouth, Danny Boy, or I might have to scold you."

Sykes took a swing at Slocum that was too fast to be dodged. Even though he'd seen it coming, Slocum was laughing too hard to keep from being knocked on the jaw.

"That's for the bullshit you said down there," Sykes snarled.

It hadn't been a very hard punch, so Slocum let it pass. "I suppose I had that coming. You're staying in this room, though, or you can sleep outside."

"What the hell for?"

"Because Corrington is probably somewhere in this hotel."

"And if he catches on that we're after him, it'll mean he'll only have one room to watch."

"If we're here long enough for him to catch on, you can have this room all to yourself. How's that strike you?"

Sykes thought about that for a spell and grudgingly picked up his saddlebags. "I'll hold you to it. I may even sleep with my damn horse."

"Go right ahead on both counts."

The room was done up with something fancy or frilly on every surface. Each piece of furniture was dusted and polished. Even the blankets on the beds were so nice that Slocum almost felt bad for setting his feet on one of them when he leaned back in one of the chairs and began sorting through the pile of books he'd bought.

"Anything good in there?" Sykes asked.

Slocum ground his teeth together while turning the pages of one particular volume. "I see why Harper's so fired up to go after me. According to this, I slaughtered entire families outside of Dallas."

"Was that before or after what you did in Fort Griffin?"

"Instead of unpacking your unmentionables, why don't you take a look around this place and see if we can find our writer friend?" Lowering the book so he could look over it to Sykes, he added, "Unless you want to spend your time sharing a room with me?"

"Hell no. I'd rather poke a rabid dog with a short stick than stay this close to you."

When Sykes marched out of the room, Slocum raised the book and continued flipping the pages. "And that," he said to himself, "is why I wanted one room."

Slocum didn't know how Sykes conducted his search, but he conducted one of his own soon after. He hadn't been there long enough to panic just yet, so he settled for walking the halls and investigating the sound of any doors being opened or shut. It was a simple system, but quickly allowed him to find out that roughly half the rooms in the hotel were rented out. Half of those were to women, and one of the remaining men was most definitely not the writer. That is, unless Edward Corrington was an old Chinese fellow who could barely walk.

Sitting at one of the small tables in the hotel's dining room, Slocum positioned himself so his back was to a wall and he was looking out at anyone who came and went. People drifted in and sat down, most of them ordering food, while others merely talked over drinks. It was all very cordial until Sykes stomped over to Slocum's table wearing a wide, self-satisfied grin.

"Found him," Sykes said proudly.

"How'd you do that?"

"Had a talk with that desk clerk. Once I got him talking about his cousin or brother or whoever the hell it was, he took a shine to me. From then on, I could have gotten him to show me the hotel's safe and let me spin the dial."

"Corrington is staying in the room two doors down the hall from ours."

Sykes looked at him as if Slocum had sprouted horns. "How do you know that?"

"I checked the register."

"That's just because I distracted the clerk."

"Sure it is," Slocum grunted.

"So you know what room he's in. Do you even know what he looks like?" Before Slocum could answer, Sykes proudly said, "Short fellow. Round face. Red hair. He sits at the same table for every meal he takes here. That table right over there, to be exact."

Snapping his head in the direction Sykes had been pointing, Slocum found a short fellow with a round face and red hair sitting with an older gentleman with a trimmed beard and three women.

Settling into his chair at the table, Sykes scooted around so he could watch the writer without being too obvious about it. "Seems like we did the same job from different angles. Maybe we should've stuck together."

"That's what I wanted to do, but figured you wouldn't have any part of it."

"Working together is one thing. Rooming together is . . . Wait a second. I think he spotted me."

"Is that a problem?" Slocum asked.

Twisting around to put his back to the writer's table, Sykes lowered his head and whispered, "He may have picked me out a few other times when I was tracking him."

"Tracking him? Through town, you mean?"

"A little. Mostly at a few stores across the street."

"Oh for Christ's sake," Slocum growled. "Haven't you ever followed someone before?"

"Well excuse the hell outta me for not being a snake in

the grass. The only time I ever trail behind someone is when I'm hunting 'em down, and it's never made any sense to lag behind for this long. Is he looking at us?"

Slocum glanced toward the writer, to find everyone at that table looking nervously in his direction. "Yeah, looks like you've spooked them all real good."

When Slocum took the napkin from his lap and threw it onto the table, Sykes asked, "What are you doing?"

Slocum pushed back from the table, stood up, and calmly started walking.

"Where are you going?" Sykes asked again, before getting up quickly enough to bump the table with his knee and rattle everything on top of it.

"I'm going over to introduce myself. Since you've done everything but mark us already, we might as well do what we came to do."

Sykes stuck his hand into his pocket to fetch the new knife he'd gotten from the old lady's store. "I was hoping to have a bit more privacy for our meeting."

"And I was hoping to handle this with a bit more discretion. Seems like neither of us can get what he wants."

With that, Slocum crossed the room and took stock of the situation. The writer was already squirming a bit, but that was probably due to the fact that Sykes was rushing to approach the table along with Slocum. The older man with the beard looked like a man of means. Not only was his silver beard trimmed into a perfect point two inches below his chin, but his tailored suit was perfectly maintained. The trio of women was also very well groomed. Two of them looked to be somewhere in their early twenties. One was a slender blonde in an expensive black dress, and the other was a brunette with thin lips, tanned skin, and a red dress. The third woman was slightly older and wrapped in velvet, which complemented hair that, depending on how the light hit it, was either dark brown or a muted shade of red. The ladies all looked at Slocum with varying degrees of interest while the two men at the table shifted uncomfortably in their seats.

"Can I . . . uhh . . . Can I help you?" the man with the round face stammered.

Holding his hat in one hand, Slocum replied with a question of his own. "Are you Edward Corrington, the writer?"

"Why, yes, I am."

Sykes stood behind Slocum, but seemed content to let him do the talking for now.

"I'm an admirer of your work," Slocum said. "Would it be too much of an imposition to join you for a few moments?"

Corrington relaxed a little when he heard that, but the sight of Sykes was obviously distracting him. "I'm speaking to my editor and some friends, but I suppose I could spare a moment."

Reaching out to drape an arm around Sykes, Slocum explained, "This is a friend of mine. He's the shy type, but don't let that bother you. He's probably been following you around like a ghoul when all he wanted was to ask for you to sign one of his books."

The sigh that Corrington let out was almost large enough to fill the sails of a seagoing vessel. "I admit, I had noticed him throughout the day. If your friend wanted a word, all he had to do was ask. Please, take a seat."

The old man huffed as if shuffling his chair over a few inches was going to be the death of him. All three women smiled politely, but stayed close enough to bask in the writer's presence. Now that he was closer, Slocum was able to take note of the writer's stocky build. His clothes didn't reek of money like the old man's, but they were better than anything Slocum carried with him. Of course, considering the few bits of clothes crumpled into his bags, that wasn't saying much.

"So what brings you to Perryville?" Corrington asked.

Sykes quickly replied, "We came to see you."

"Did you, now? Well that's very flattering."

The woman with the possibly red hair tapped on Corrington's elbow and whispered into his ear while looking across the table at Slocum. Patting her on the arm and nodding, Corrington announced, "My manners are appalling. Let me introduce you to the rest of my table. This is Jessica, Hannah, and Rose." In order, those names belonged to the redhead, the blonde, and the brunette with the thin lips. "And this," the writer said while patting the older man on the back, "is my editor, Walter Saunders. He came all the way out from the East Coast to wish me well on my tour along the Mississippi River."

Walter stood up just enough to acknowledge the other two men, but not enough to fully clear his seat.

"How far east?" Slocum asked.

"Boston," Walter replied. "Our little publishing house is quite proud of Edward's success. The least we could do was accompany him on his little expedition."

"Have you made it up to Chicago yet?" Slocum asked.

The writer shook his head and picked up the drink that had been sitting on the table in front of him. "Not yet."

"I heard there was some trouble there," Sykes said.

If those words struck any chord with the writer, Corrington was real good at keeping it hidden as he extended a hand toward his guests and raised his eyebrows expectantly. "And by what name shall I call you?"

"I'm John Slocum."

Those words did cause the color to drain from Corrington's face.

"And I'm Daniel Sykes. Perhaps you've heard of us?"

16

Slocum could feel the writer's palm growing slick within his grasp as he continued to shake Corrington's hand. Even after Slocum let go and sat down, the writer seemed unable to pull his arm back.

"That's rich," Walter said. "Aren't those the names you used for some of your books?"

Without looking at the well-dressed editor, Slocum replied, "They sure are, except I've had that name a lot longer than he's been using it."

"And we sure don't appreciate you draggin' our names through the mud like you have," Sykes added.

Walter showed more of a spark as he laughed and dabbed at his brow with a napkin. "Are you telling me those are truly your names? What a remarkable coincidence!"

"That's not what I would call it," Slocum said evenly.

Although the two men in front of Slocum were having mixed reactions, the three women all seemed to be of the same mind. They watched Slocum and Sykes with growing interest. Jessica even leaned away from Corrington so she could get that much closer to Slocum. It was only a difference of a few inches, but the change spoke volumes about what was going through her mind. The other two likewise diverted some of the admiration they'd been casting at the writer toward the two characters who'd sought him out.

It had taken a while, but Walter was finally getting the idea that all was not well at the table. His chuckles became less and less humorous as he took notice of the way the other three men were staring at each other. "Those were fictional characters in your books, right, Edward?"

When Edward started to speak, Slocum stared at him even harder. The message was conveyed well enough for the writer to lean back as though he'd been shoved. "Perhaps this isn't the best time to discuss such things. After all, confidentiality and everything."

"Confidentiality?" Walter huffed. "In regards to what? I'd like an answer to my question." When he didn't get one, he looked over to the other two. "Are you men saying you are the actual people depicted in Edward's books?"

All three women watched with growing interest. Jessica even brushed her fingertips along the side of her neck as she waited for a response.

"You think my friend and me could have a word with Edward alone?" Sykes asked. "I bet we could straighten all of this out real quick."

Walter pushed his chair away from the table and stood up. "The quicker the better. I'll return in a moment."

Slocum stood up as well as he said, "Excuse us, ladies, but Edward and I have some matters to discus."

"Oh, don't mind us," Jessica quickly said. "We won't interfere."

Before Slocum could respond, Sykes was up and coming around the table toward Corrington. "Things may get a little messy. Wouldn't want to ruin any of those pretty dresses."

Corrington couldn't get any paler, but he was trembling and was too weak to resist when Slocum took hold of him by the arm and led him out of the room. "Don't pay any mind to Danny," he said. "He runs his mouth too much."

By the time he was able to form words, Corrington was stumbling out the front door of the hotel. The cool September air invigorated him enough to say, "Whatever this is about, I'm sure we can settle it amicably."

"You know damn well what this is about," Sykes said.

After rounding a corner, Slocum pushed the writer toward the hotel until Corrington's back knocked against the building's side wall. The street was nearby, but was practically deserted. The few folks walking along the boardwalk on the opposite side were too wrapped up in their own affairs to listen when Slocum said, "You've got some things to answer for, Mr. Corrington."

Sykes stood between the writer and the street. His hand came up to flick the pocketknife open with a quick snap of his wrist. "You sure as hell do, and now's the time to take care of our business."

Corrington barely caught sight of the blade before Slocum grabbed Sykes by the wrist and forced him to lower it. Even that quick glimpse of sharpened steel was enough to take the wind from the writer's sails. He slumped back against the wall and let out a moaning breath. If Slocum hadn't been quick enough to pin him to the wall by pressing his hand flat against his chest, Corrington would have dropped straight to the ground.

"Why'd you write that trash about us?" Slocum asked.

The writer's head lolled from side to side as he struggled to remain conscious. "They were . . . just books. Just stories."

"Stories about me. About Dan here. Didn't you think folks would read those stories?"

"Honestly? I didn't think *so many* would read them. My books never sold so well until I . . . ."

"Until you what?" Slocum asked. "Until you started using real names and passing the stories off as fact?"

Snapping awake in an instant, Corrington steadied himself as best he could when he said, "I never passed them off as fact!"

"Tell that to the bounty hunters that're using those yellowback novels to justify hunting us down."

"Don't you already have a price on your head, Mr. Slocum?" Corrington asked. "According to my research—"

Stopping the writer by slamming him against the wall, Slocum said, "You don't know shit about me or what I done. And don't stand there trying to tell me that I murdered innocent folks in Fort Griffin." Seeing the guilty shadow that fell over Corrington's face, Slocum nodded and moved even closer to him. "Did you really think you could spout off like that in print and nothing would come of it?"

"I think he did," Sykes said. Holding the pocketknife up so the little blade was at the writer's eye level, he added, "But something sure is gonna come of it. There's a price that's gotta be paid."

"My research," Corrington croaked. "According to my research, those incidents are said to have happened."

"I don't know where the hell you got that stuff about me in Fort Griffin, but it's gotten some men riled up. You wrote there's a price on my head linked to that lie."

"And there is a price on your head," Corrington was quick to say. "Just not exactly as I depicted. But I do my research! I put together bits and pieces of rumor, legend, and some fact to make a good story. That's what I do! That's all I do. I'm a writer!"

"How are folks supposed to know what's true and what you made up?" Sykes asked.

"They could start by reading my book!" When he saw the little blade move closer to his face, Corrington squirmed to get away from it. "It's right there in the front of every book. Under the acknowledgments. I state it all very plainly."

Sykes grabbed hold of the writer's collar and leaned in while cocking his knife hand back like an arrow that was about to be launched. "To hell with this!"

"Wait!" Slocum warned. His gun hand was quick enough to snap up and out in time to slap against Sykes's wrist as it lunged forward. Sykes's blade was diverted, but there was enough muscle behind it to drive it an inch or so into the wall a hairsbreadth from Corrington's left ear.

Although Sykes cursed at him while trying to pull the blade from where it had been lodged, Slocum removed the book he'd carried in his pocket and flipped it open. When he saw the acknowledgment page, he skimmed the words and then held the book so Sykes could get a look at it. "It's right here."

"I don't give a damn what that says. That asshole ain't got the right to use our names like that."

"I swear," Corrington said, "it wasn't my intention to cause any harm. I even thanked you whenever possible. I went out of my way to make it clear that you were merely inspiration."

"Well some of the men who read your books didn't pay attention to that part," Slocum pointed out.

"There are some crazy people out there."

"Is that why you brought armed men along with you?"

Corrington was caught off guard by that. And, judging by the expression on his face, so was Sykes. "What armed men?" he asked.

Slocum kept his eyes fixed solidly on Corrington when he said, "The ones that Walter went to get when he excused himself. I guess you didn't really plan on needing to bring gunmen along for dinner with an old man and three women, did you?"

"Wh-why would I?" Corrington sheepishly replied. He started to say something else, but was silenced when Slocum clapped his hand over his mouth.

Around the front of the hotel, a door opened and a man called out, "Edward? You out here?"

Slocum pressed his hand against the writer's mouth, but

he could feel the scream building up inside of the smaller man. If Corrington decided to draw attention to himself, it wouldn't take much. There were plenty of ways to keep him quiet, but Slocum wasn't quite ready to follow through on anything so drastic.

Extending his arm, Sykes pressed the blade of his pocket-knife flat against the writer's face just below his eye. He flashed his teeth in something close to an animal's snarl before putting a finger of his free hand up to his lips in a shushing motion.

Corrington was too petrified to inhale, let alone defy both of his captors.

A few seconds later, Walter said something to whoever was with him and shut the door.

Slocum eased Sykes's hand back and slowly lowered his own. "We don't want to hurt you, mister. If that's what we'd wanted, you would have been dead already."

"Yes," Corrington gasped. "I figured as much."

"And what makes you such a goddamn expert on what we're capable of?" Sykes demanded angrily.

Corrington shrugged and said, "I've done my research. I've written your character through four books. I know what kind of dastardly things a truly wicked man can do."

Slocum had to laugh at how far off and almost dead-on that comment was. "The reason we came to see you is to let you know that you can't use us in your books anymore. You're a writer, so make something up. Why even use our names if you aren't going to be truthful?"

No matter what else was going on, Corrington had to smirk at that. "That's a bit of a naïve thing to say. Your name is a known quantity and that made for some pretty good sales."

"Well tough shit, because those sales are over."

"Wait a second," Sykes cut in. "What did he call us? Ny-eve?"

"It means stupid," Slocum said, even though he knew better. As he'd expected, that wiped away the smugness that had just started taking root on Corrington's face.

"No, no," the writer said as the blade pressed into his cheek. "I meant to say—"

"What he meant to say is that he's going to fix the damage he's done," Slocum interrupted. "Isn't that right?"

"Sure," Corrington replied. "Only . . . how would you propose I do that?"

When Slocum let him go, he did so with another shove that almost knocked the wind out of Corrington's lungs. "Ain't my problem. You're the fellow with the big imagination. Think of something."

The front door opened again and several people came outside calling the writer by name. "Are you sure he's supposed to be out here?" a man asked.

"Yes," Walter replied. "The lady at the front desk said she saw Edward go outside and that he was escorted by those two others."

"Maybe they went to get a drink."

"You think that's why I called you down? Because I was worried they'd be getting drinks?"

As the conversation continued just around the corner of the building, Corrington glanced back and forth between Slocum and Sykes. "That would be my editor and the men he hired to protect me. I should probably go back before they get too anxious."

"Go on," Slocum told him. "But I'll be expecting a resolution to this problem very soon. If I don't get it, no amount of hired hands are going to keep me from knocking you down and letting him skin you alive."

Sykes liked the sound of that and showed it by grinning while flipping the pocketknife in the air and catching it like a lucky coin.

"I suppose I could print some sort of retraction."

"You'll do better than that," Sykes said. "You'll call off them bounty hunters that your books put on our trail."

"Edward?" the men around the front of the building hollered. They were spreading out down the street and approaching the side of the building where Slocum had brought the writer for their chat.

"I didn't tell any bounty hunters to go after you," Corrington insisted.

Although the writer didn't seem like he was going to bolt, Slocum knew his audience with the man wasn't going to last for much longer. So, instead of concerning himself with staying hidden, he opted to get as much done in as little time as possible. "You won't mention our names in one more book, you got that?"

"Yes, sir. Of course."

Slocum looked toward the street to see if anyone searching for the writer was about to stumble upon him. What he saw was a glint of light from the hotel and street lanterns being reflected off of a gun barrel poking only an inch or so out of a second-floor window of the building across the street. Taking both hands away from Corrington and stepping back, he said, "Better call off your men before somebody gets hurt."

Corrington drew a breath to call out, but the rifle across the street sent its round through the air with a sharp crack. A single bullet hissed toward the building and clipped the brim of Slocum's hat. Sykes leapt straight back to press his shoulders against the side of the neighboring building as Slocum grabbed onto Corrington's shirt.

"Call 'em off!" Slocum demanded.

"Walter only brought two guards and they stay with him!"

"Edward?" Walter shouted from the street. "Are you shot?"

It didn't take much to spot the confusion on the writer's face and hear the panic in Walter's voice. Those two things most certainly did not add up to one of the writer's own men firing at them. Drawing his pistol, Slocum rushed toward the rear of the hotel and shoved Corrington ahead of him as another rifle round punched into the hotel's wall. Sykes was coming along with him, trotting backward while raising his gun hand to sight along the top of his .44.

"Put that gun down, you damn fool," Slocum demanded.

Sykes kept the pistol raised, but didn't squeeze his trigger. "They shot first!"

"Doesn't matter. We came into this town to stop being portrayed as mad-dog killers, not to play up to the role by firing into dark windows."

"So what would you have us do?" Sykes asked.

Once they reached the back of the hotel, Slocum shoved Corrington toward Sykes. "Keep him from getting hurt and make it seem like we're both back here, angry as a pair of wet hens." While skirting along the back of the next building, Slocum added, "Just make a whole lot of noise. That shouldn't be too hard for you."

Sykes watched as Slocum drew his Colt and ran along the back side of the neighboring building. From there, he circled around the next corner to disappear from his sight. Judging by what he knew of the street and where the shots had come from, Sykes figured Slocum would be in a prime spot to flank the rifleman as long as he wasn't spotted first.

"You heard the man," Sykes said with a wild grin. "Let's make some noise." Before Corrington could protest, Sykes aimed in the general direction of the source of the rifle fire and pulled his trigger. Not only did that spark some shouting from the street, but it brought a whole salvo of gunfire into the alley.

Corrington huddled down and covered his head with both hands. He may have been muttering to himself, but Sykes couldn't make out what was said over the thunder of the gunshots.

"You'll never take me alive!" Sykes shouted.

That brought Corrington's head up faster than a prairie dog poking its head from its hole. "What?"

After firing again, Sykes shrugged and said, "Never mind that. Got carried away is all."

More shots came from the street, chipping at the side of the building the rifleman had been using as his vantage point. Someone in that building must have opened a door or brought a lantern into the room because the rifleman's face was illuminated just enough for it to be seen from outside. Michael Harper leaned out through the window, levered in another round, and was quickly distracted by something from within his room. Even after Harper turned away from the window, Corrington stared up at him with wide, unblinking eyes.

"You remember what I said about crazy people being out there?" the writer asked.

Sykes took advantage of the lull in firing to replace his spent rounds with fresh bullets from his gun belt. "Yeah."

"Well I know that man with the rifle, and he's one of the craziest I've ever seen."

17

After Slocum ducked around the corner of the building next to the hotel, he didn't stop running until he'd crossed the street and gotten around behind the source of the rifle shots. He didn't slow down enough to discover if the building was a store, a home, or even a smaller hotel with cheaper rates looking to collect business from the folks who couldn't afford to stay at the Ole Miss. The only thing that Slocum cared about was the narrow set of stairs leading up from the back lot to a door on the second floor. He bounded up those two at a time, tried the door, and found it was locked. Bringing his right knee up to his chest, Slocum sent that foot straight out to smash the door in.

The room was the same width as a closet and about twice as long. At the other end was another door which wasn't locked. Slocum emerged from that one to run smack into a fellow wearing long underwear and carrying a shotgun.

"What the hell is—" was all the partially dressed man could say before Slocum took the shotgun away from him and moved down the hall.

There were two doors at that end of the hall, either one

of which could lead to a room containing the window that the rifleman had used. Slocum shouldered open the first door and swung the shotgun around to cover his entrance.

All he found inside was a single old woman curled up under several blankets, trembling like a leaf.

"Sorry about that, ma'am," Slocum said as he stepped out of the room and shut the door.

Without wasting another moment, he kicked open the next door and hopped away just in time to avoid the shot that hissed into the hallway. Slocum figured that room was fairly similar to the old woman's, which meant the window was almost directly across from the doorway.

Harper exploded from the room, swinging the rifle like a club. Apparently, he'd done some figuring of his own and decided that Slocum was most likely standing right beside the door and about to come inside. He'd been partially right, although Slocum had been kneeling instead of standing. The rifle cracked against the wall over his head, sending chunks of plaster onto Slocum's hat and shoulders.

The bounty hunter rushed down the hallway while shoving fresh rounds into the rifle so he could use it properly. With his hands full and precious little time to work with, Slocum aimed low with the shotgun and pulled one of the two triggers. The slap of metal against metal was the worst possible thing he could have heard.

For Harper, it was a choir of angels. He knew better than to savor the moment for too long, however, and turned a corner in the hallway while slipping the last round into his rifle.

"No shells?" Slocum growled as he passed the man who huddled against the wall in his long johns.

The disheveled man muttered something to Slocum as his shotgun was tossed to the floor.

Slocum arrived at the bend in the hallway, realizing he hadn't even seen it earlier when he'd come in through the nearby door. The blinders he'd been wearing then had made it so he could only see what had become a prime spot for a quick ambush. Hoping that Harper was just as anxious as he was, Slocum removed his hat and stuck it around the corner.

Sure enough, the move was answered by a sharp crack from the rifle. Slocum crouched down as low as he could while taking a gander around the corner. There was one shut door between him and the top of a staircase. Harper knelt as if he was in the front row of an army firing line. He took one quick shot, which was thrown off in his haste to lower his aim to Slocum's level. His odds of hitting anything were lessened even more when Slocum dove chest-first to the floor and slid along the hall.

The Colt Navy barked once, tearing a nasty chunk from the banister to Harper's left. Twisting on the balls of his feet, Harper shifted the rifle to his left hand and scrambled down the stairs. His right hand went to the holster under his arm, to draw the .32 he kept there, before he swung his arm up and back to fire a quick shot over his shoulder.

With nowhere to go at that particular moment, Slocum could only twitch at the sound of the shot and pray Harper wasn't lucky enough to hit anything.

The wild shot cracked a few boards in the wall, but remained lodged there without having drawn a drop of blood.

"Get the hell out of my place!" the man in long johns said over the distinctive click of a shotgun's breech being closed.

Slocum fired his Colt and moved toward the top of the stairs. Harper had already gone down to the first floor, and his steps were carrying him through the house in a direction that would probably take him to a back door.

Outside, a few more shots crackled in the street. At one point, Slocum swore he heard Sykes shouting like a mad-dog bank robber being chased by a posse. Instead of trying to figure that out, Slocum kept his eyes and ears open for any sign that Harper might double back. The footsteps he'd been following echoed through the first floor of what looked to be a house or some sort of parlor. With no light apart from what trickled in from outside, Slocum could only see a few little tables and some chairs scattered within several good-sized rooms.

Suddenly, a figure stepped in front of him to fill Slocum's entire line of sight. He couldn't make out a face from the shadows, but he could see the arm that was being swung at him like a club. Slocum ducked under it and charged forward to try and knock the figure out of his way.

At the last moment, the figure twisted to get out of Slocum's path. A hand dropped heavily onto Slocum's back, grabbed his clothes, and swung him so his own momentum carried him into one of those chairs he'd just spotted.

Once his legs became entangled and he lost his balance, Slocum had a tough time figuring out which way was up. He knew he'd lost his footing, but the blows he felt against his ribs, stomach, chest, and back could have come from someone hitting him or just his body falling against more chairs. Even after Slocum's back hit the floor, the room still felt as if it was turning around him. Not even blinking or rubbing his eyes did him much good, since the room was just as dark either way.

As the figure loomed over him, Slocum lifted his gun hand so he could protect himself. Almost immediately, a boot stomped down to pin that wrist to the floor. He could feel the weight against his arm increase as the man bent over to get a better look at him.

"Well, well," James sneered. "I didn't think we'd draw you out so quickly. Sometimes I don't mind bein' wrong."

Rather than swap threats with the pimp, Slocum reached down with his free hand to draw the thick-bladed knife from the top of his right boot and slash at the leg that was holding him down.

James howled like a wounded animal and hopped back. The instant the weight was off of him, Slocum scrambled to his feet. Every movement was a painful reminder of the fall he'd taken only a few seconds ago, but it would have taken a lot more than that to keep him down. "So you're working with Harper now? Talk about the blind leading the blind."

Slocum could hear the other man breathing heavily as his body swayed from side to side. After taking half a step forward with one foot, James lunged on the other at a slightly different angle. The first half step got Slocum to jump a bit faster than he should have, and James caught him with a glancing knee. The impact knocked the gun from Slocum's hand to hit the floor with a heavy thump. With all the shadows in that room, the Colt Navy might as well have fallen to the bottom of a murky pool.

Considering all the abuse his body had taken thus far, a little bit more wasn't going to put Slocum down. On the contrary, he used that to spur him on as he straightened up and pounded his forearm into James's chest.

The other man reeled back while swinging wildly. One fist knocked Slocum's hat from his head while the other clipped him on the cheek.

Slocum continued wrestling until he managed to put some space between himself and James. Adding to that space by taking a step back, Slocum now had enough room to take a short swing at James. The boot knife sliced through the air and tore through the other man's shirt. James yelped, slapped Slocum's arm away, and reached for the gun at his hip.

When guns were brought into a fight, every second became precious. Since his Colt was out of reach, Slocum came up with a little something he knew about James involving a bullet that had ripped through his left shoulder back in Chicago. He flipped the knife to his right hand and pounded its handle against that shoulder.

"Son of a BITCH!" James shouted, letting Slocum know he'd remembered correctly as to which shoulder had been wounded.

The pain was overpowering enough that James had to

fight to keep from crumpling over. He grabbed his shoulder, forgetting about everything else for a few seconds, until the flaring agony subsided. Never one to allow a good opportunity to pass, Slocum was ready to make sure James didn't bother him again.

"Not another move!" the man in long johns shouted.

With the man's voice still echoing through the room, Slocum took a quick look over at the dim glow of light coming from the doorway. The man held a lantern in one hand and his shotgun in the other, both of which were trembling with nervous anticipation.

"Before you get your courage up," the man warned, "you should know I had plenty of time to shove a few loads of buckshot into this gun."

Since the man looked nervous enough already, Slocum doubted he had the sand to try and bluff two armed men. "I'm warnin' you!" the man squawked with more than enough conviction to convince Slocum his claim was genuine.

"All right," Slocum said as he eased the knife back into its scabbard. "I'm unarmed."

"Now get the hell out of my place. Right now!"

Slocum and James looked at each other for a few seconds. In that time, they both strained under the mounting pain of their bumps and bruises. Motioning toward the back door, which was visible thanks to the bit of moonlight spilling in through a rear window, James said, "After you."

"Oh, no," the man with the shotgun warned. "I don't want anyone killing someone inside my place, and I don't want anyone getting killed on my property neither. One of you will go out the back and the other will go out the front. If'n I see either of you lingering for too long, I'll start shooting."

Like a dog baring its teeth when its dinner is threatened, James started reaching for a weapon.

Slocum wasn't going to stand still for the other man, so he started moving toward his Colt, which he'd finally spotted on the floor.

"You're lingering," the man in long johns said.

"Fine," James spat. "It's not like you can get too far away anyhow, Slocum."

"I've got no reason to run. If you and Harper are in town, everything I want is right here."

Before he could be warned again, James threw a disgruntled wave at both other men and stomped toward the back door.

"Now you," the other man said.

Slocum picked up his Colt and walked toward the front door. The shotgunner warned him to leave the gun where it was, but after all that had happened, Slocum simply wasn't frightened of one man in his underwear. On his way out, Slocum listened for what was going on in the street. He could only hear a few raised voices and some horses passing by, which meant the fighting was over. James had slithered away like the snake he was. If he'd decided to continue his bout with Slocum, he surely would have announced himself by now.

A small group had gathered in front of the Ole Miss Wheelhouse. Upon seeing Slocum emerge from the doorway across the street, that group commenced to chattering among themselves at a furious pace. He wasn't about to join them, but since they were in front of the hotel he couldn't exactly avoid them. It was a blessing for him when Slocum caught a glimpse of Sykes standing well away from the gossips, waving furiously to catch his attention.

After nodding at Sykes to get him to stop waving, Slocum walked slowly toward the hotel. He made sure to look as many of the gossips directly in the eyes as he could before scattering them like birds from a bush when he casually rested his hand on the holstered Colt at his side. Once there wasn't much of anyone left to watch where he was going, Slocum changed direction and walked down the street.

It wasn't long before he heard Sykes whispering, "Over here."

Sykes had moved to a different spot, but he wasn't trying to hide. After Slocum chose a post at the corner of the boardwalk, he leaned against it and fished a cigarette from his shirt pocket. By the time he struck a match against the weathered post, Sykes and Corrington were close enough for their faces to catch the flickering light.

"I trust the two of you are unscathed," Slocum said.

Corrington sputtered something that made him sound like a faulty steam valve.

"Just some ruffled feathers," Sykes told him. "What about you?"

"I was able to sneak up on that rifleman. Turns out he's—"

"Mike Harper," Corrington said. He then clamped his lips shut and nervously glanced around as if speaking that name in the open was enough to summon the devil himself.

Clenching his teeth around the cigarette almost hard enough to snip all the way through it, Slocum asked, "You know him?"

Corrington nodded nervously. "I was telling Mr. Sykes about him."

"Well go on and tell John. He'll want to hear."

"He came to the event I planned for the release of one of my books. See, I figured I'd try to make a commotion about the releases instead of just letting them go out and do their best unannounced. I find it gives them more of a . . ." Catching the impatient glare that was boiling within Slocum's eyes, Corrington cleared his throat and said, "I've been doing a lot of traveling, hosting several of these events, and Mike Harper has been showing up at more and more of them. Every time, he talks to me at length about my works as if he thinks they're factual accounts."

"Would you imagine that?" Slocum said sarcastically. "I bet that didn't work out too well for you."

"It most certainly did not," Corrington replied. "When he told me he was resigning from his job as a telegraph clerk to become a bounty hunter, I merely thought he was telling me a story. When he came back wearing a gun and saying he'd devoted his life to hunting down the men in my books, I became worried. That's when my editor insisted on hiring men to come along with me for protection."

"Why didn't you just stop all this gallivanting around?"

Corrington drew a sharp breath as if he'd just gotten stabbed through the chest. "Stop spreading the word about my books?"

"If it means staying out of the sights of men like Harper? Yeah."

"Do you know how difficult it is to make a living writing those books? Only now after my parties and appearances have I been making a real name for myself. I've never seen profit like this!"

"And you may not see much of anything," Slocum pointed out, "if Harper gets you killed."

"I think he was trying to protect me. Once I have a word with him, rationally of course, I can more than likely convince him of his error in coming after you men."

"Rational," Sykes muttered. "I'm sure that's exactly what Harper is."

Despite the unmistakable nature of Sykes's barbed comment, Corrington didn't take much notice of it. Instead, he started walking toward the Ole Miss and then sharply came to a halt. "Is it safe to return, John?"

"As safe as it's ever going to be for us," Slocum replied.

Once again, Corrington either missed or decided to ignore the real meaning being conveyed and strolled along the side of the street as if he was just out to fill his lungs with some cool night air.

"He ain't right in the head, is he?" Sykes asked.

"Haven't you read any of those books?"

"I see your point. I suppose I should stay with him. If anyone's gonna be able to set Harper straight or at least put him off our tails, it'd be him."

Slocum reached out to grab Sykes's elbow and kept him from getting too far away. "It's not just Harper we need to worry about," he said in a voice that was quiet enough to remain mostly between them. "He was with another gunman that crossed my path in Chicago."

"Who is he?"

"Just some pimp with a mean streak, but he's armed and doesn't mind spilling blood. If he's here, I'm guessing his partner is as well. That one's a younger fella who'll probably bolt once the going gets tough."

"I take it you ran afoul of these two somehow?" Sykes asked.

"You could say that. I called them out in front of the whole city, whipped them in a place they'd staked out as their own, and watched as their friend was gunned down."

"You killed their friend?"

"No," Slocum replied, "but I doubt they're willing to overlook that part."

Sykes slapped his hands together and strutted after Corrington. "Just when I think we got this bronco roped, it just keeps on kickin'!"

18

Slocum sat in his room, weighing his options.

On one hand, he could see this thing through and make sure that Harper didn't get away with the trespasses he'd already made and that James would be denied the bragging rights he'd earn by chasing down John Slocum and living to tell the tale. On the other hand, Sykes had a point. Just when he thought this whole affair was about to be finished, something else came along to spur it along. Nobody was forcing Slocum to stay. In fact, he'd been planning on heading out west, where the land felt more open and a man could watch the sunsets while troubles from his past melted away. That's the line of reasoning that filled so many wagon trains and boomtowns, after all.

It was also the kind of reasoning that allowed men like James and Harper to build themselves up as soon as someone like Slocum lowered his guard.

Just thinking about those two stoked the fire in Slocum's belly. Walking away was too damn close to throwing his hands up and letting them win. James would probably get a thrill out of that and use it to put a fright into his working girls or anyone who tried to entice them away from him. Harper wasn't the sort who would let the matter drop, though. As far as that went, neither was Slocum.

Outlaws had to see the matter through because they worked like a pack of wolves. A sign of weakness from one was akin to baring his throat to an anxious male looking to take the pack for himself. The life Slocum led put him in a similar circumstance. If young gunhands looking to make a name for themselves thought he was an easy mark, they would keep coming.

On a more personal note, Slocum had simply been pushed too far to let it go. No matter how morally right it might have been to take the high road and walk away, he simply wouldn't have been able to look himself in a mirror again knowing he'd rolled over for the likes of Michael Harper.

"God damn it," he snarled as he grabbed the bottle of whiskey he'd brought with him all the way from Chicago.

Sitting in that room, he felt like he was hiding.

Slocum knew that wasn't the case, but he wanted to charge out, pull Harper from wherever he was keeping himself, and pound his face into mush for all the shots he'd taken at him. Somehow, finding out that Harper was unhinged made matters even worse. Slocum may not have liked or respected bounty hunters, but he knew what was going through their minds when they went after someone. A man who was touched in the head didn't need a reason to start something, and he probably wouldn't stop until he was dead. It also meant such a man could be unpredictable enough to get ahead of any man thinking along straight lines.

Now that Slocum knew what he was dealing with, he could act accordingly. "All right then," he said while sloshing the remaining whiskey around in its bottle. "You want a hunt? That's what you'll get. Come hunt me down and see what happens."

When someone knocked on his door, Slocum nearly

dropped his whiskey. He sat in his chair with his feet still propped on the bed, staring at the door as though he'd been caught red-handed after a robbery.

The knock came again, but was harder and a little quicker.

"Yeah?" Slocum grunted.

"Mr. Slocum?"

"That's right."

"Could you open the door please?"

From what he'd heard, Slocum could tell two things. The person on the other side of that door was a woman, and she was in a hurry. He drew his gun and approached the door, careful not to stand directly in front of it. Men like Harper and especially James weren't above shooting some holes through a closed door just to win their fight.

"What do you want?" Slocum asked through the wooden barrier.

Lowering her voice a bit, she replied, "I'd rather not discuss it in the hallway."

Slocum opened the door just enough to get a look at Jessica standing in front of him. The moment she saw his face, she showed him an anxious smile and said, "Please let me in."

Slocum stepped aside without a word so she could hurry into his room. She was in a different dress than she'd been wearing earlier that night at Corrington's table. Instead of the expensive-looking velvet number, she was now wrapped in black lace and silk that clung to her upper body like a second skin and blossomed nicely at the hips, without the need of a bustle.

"So what's the big hurry?" he asked. "Did someone tell you a writer was in here?"

"Not hardly. I was told you were in here. Looks like my sources were right."

Slocum didn't even bother asking about her sources. If there was yet another person keeping track of his every move, he didn't want to hear about it. Holding out the bottle, he asked, "Care for a drink? You might want to take it before it's all gone."

"No," she replied while gliding up to stand close enough to press her firm breasts against him. "That's not why I came here."

"Don't tell me Corrington sent you."

She laughed under her breath at that. "He writes about a lot of exciting things. I read every single one of his books. Even though other women look at me funny for reading them instead of Shakespeare or whatever other high-minded garbage they think will make them look smart. I prefer to read about exciting men. The sort of men Eddie always writes about." Lowering her eyes to drink in the sight of him while her hands roamed freely over Slocum's chest, she said, "But you're the real thing aren't you, Mr. Slocum? Just like in Eddie's books?"

Until now, Slocum had gotten nothing but grief for being the subject of that yellowback trash. So if a very nice little perk to being in those books was going to come along, he wasn't about to turn his nose up at it. Slocum holstered his gun so he could put both of his hands on Jessica's hips.

"That's right, miss," he told her. "Just like in those books."

She lapped that up like a dish of warm milk. Her fingers curled so her nails dragged against his chest as she slid her hands down to his belt. While unbuckling it, she looked into his eyes and then lunged forward to plant a hard kiss on his lips. Slocum barely had a chance to catch his breath before Jessica chewed on his bottom lip and pulled his jeans down just far enough for her to get her hand into them.

"Just as I imagined when I read about you," she whispered. His cock was growing hard in her grasp, and she stroked it until it ached to be in her.

Slocum grabbed her by the arms and pulled her dress down off her shoulders to bare her breasts. She arched her back and let out a moan when he cupped her tits and massaged them until her nipples were just as hard as what she had in her hand.

"I've been thinking about this ever since *Six-Gun Devil*."

Normally, hearing the title of that book would have clawed at Slocum's patience and twisted his guts into a knot. But when Jessica mentioned it, she was also lowering herself to her knees and tugging his jeans all the way down to his ankles. Her lips wrapped around his rigid pole and her tongue slid along its entire length as she sucked him from base to tip. Looking up at him, she held him in her hand and said, "Sit on the bed."

He was happy to comply. Along the way, he shed most of his clothes and kicked off his boots. Sitting on the edge of the bed, Slocum watched as she stood up and peeled off her dress to reveal a body that was even better than he'd imagined. Her hips were small and her stomach was flat. Jessica's breasts were plump and pendulous, swaying perfectly as she stepped up to the bed and knelt in front of him.

Her hands slid beneath her tits, cupping them while teasing her nipples with the occasional fingertip. Leaning forward, she placed Slocum's cock between her breasts and started moving up and down. "You like that?" she asked.

Slocum grabbed her and held onto her breasts so they wrapped tighter around him. Her skin was soft and warm, but not nearly as warm as where he wanted to be.

"Get up here," he told her.

"So strong and demanding," she sighed as she climbed onto the bed and straddled him. When Slocum leaned back, she mounted his cock and impaled herself on it. Jessica's hand lingered between her legs, massaging the sensitive nub of flesh just above the spot where he entered her. "God, this is just as good as I imagined."

Once she settled so her breasts were brushing against his chest, Slocum wrapped his arms around her and said, "It's about to get a whole lot better." With that, he began pumping up into her in strong, solid movements.

Every time he buried his cock between her legs, Jessica gasped and moaned. Slocum only did that a few more times before he began to stay inside for only seconds, then slowly ease back out. After she'd caught her breath, Jessica placed her hands flat on his chest and gathered her legs beneath her body so she was squatting on top of him.

"My turn," she said as she began moving straight up and down.

The muscles in her legs were like iron, and she rode him without any sign of letting up. Jessica threw her head back and started to shudder once she found just the right way to move. Eventually, she settled on top of him so he was all the way inside and began pumping her hips furiously back and forth.

Slocum grabbed onto her hips, but he wasn't about to do anything that might break her stride. She was doing just fine on her own. In fact, the intense pleasure on her face was quite a sight. When she climaxed, her eyes snapped open and her hands pressed down hard against Slocum's chest. Her legs closed tightly on either side of his body and she let out a soft moan that could barely be heard.

He could feel when her storm had passed, which was when Slocum rolled her onto her back and settled in between her thighs. She spread her legs open wide for him and accepted his rigid cock gratefully. Slocum ran his hand along one of her muscled legs and was glad to feel her lift it up for him. That little shift allowed him to drive even deeper into her with every stroke.

Kneeling between her legs, Slocum cupped her ass and hung on as he thrust in and out of her. When he leaned forward again, both of his hands settled on her breasts so he could knead the soft mounds as he built to his own climax. He lay on top of her, took her hands, and pinned them to the bed, so Jessica's arms were stretched up over her head.

She lay there as if she was chained to a wall, watching him with excited eyes and wriggling her body in time to his movements.

The sight of her beneath him was almost enough to push Slocum over the edge. Jessica's breasts shook with the impact of his body against hers. Her hair was a wild mess splayed out under her head, and even when he moved his hands down to massage the front of her body, she kept her arms stretched in the spot where he'd placed them. Jessica writhed contentedly, giving in to the next wave of pleasure to wash through her. When Slocum exploded inside of her, she gasped and moaned. Before he could move away, she ground her hips against him, straining for every last second she could get out of him.

He stayed where he was for as long as he could. Finally, he had to collapse on the bed next to her. "You're gonna wear me down to the bone," he said.

Lying on her side, Jessica rubbed his chest and told him, "I haven't had enough of you yet."

"Well, this'll have to do until I catch my breath."

She was obviously disappointed, but she nestled against him.

After a little bit of sleep, Slocum awoke to find her naked body still curled up beside him. She'd flipped over onto her other side, so she was now facing away. When she stirred, her smooth rump brushed against his groin. If she'd meant to arouse him, she'd done a hell of a good job. If the timing of her movement had just been a happy accident, well Slocum was fine with that as well.

"What are you doing?" she asked sleepily.

Slocum's hand moved over her side, down to her hip, and then back up again before reaching around to rub her breasts. When he teased her nipple between his thumb and forefinger, it grew hard right away. "Would you rather I go back to sleep?" he asked.

"Not at all." She lifted one leg up and back so it was resting on Slocum's hip. Then Jessica positioned herself so she could reach down and guide him between her thighs.

At first, Slocum didn't think he could get to her. But with a few more subtle shifts of Jessica's body, he soon felt the warm dampness of her pussy against his hard pole. She made a soft purring sound as she showed him the way inside. Slocum pumped into her, feeling a whole new set of pleasures as he entered her from that angle. And he wasn't the only one to be worked up so quickly. Jessica's entire body shook in a matter of minutes, as a series of little orgasms pulsed through her one after the other. Slocum couldn't recall the last time he'd felt a woman do that. Rather than question it, he held onto her and thrust into her again and again.

Just when it seemed she would collapse from exhaustion, Jessica scooted away, flipped around to face him, and pushed Slocum onto his back. From there, she crawled on top of him, eased his cock up into her, and then started grinding her hips. Instead of riding him as she'd done earlier, she lay on top of him and simply moved her hips in various ways.

Sometimes she pumped them back and forth, but mostly it was in circles, massaging his cock with her wet pussy until it was Slocum's turn to collapse.

"Jesus Christ," he sighed.

Jessica smiled and watched him.

All Slocum could do was run his hands along her body and feel every last one of her movements. She seemed to know right when to speed up again, sapping every last bit of his strength.

Slocum woke up when he was jostled in his bed. Opening his eyes, he still felt weak as he shifted around to find Jessica sitting naked on the edge of the mattress. He watched her for a little while as she eased into her clothes layer by layer. She didn't notice she had an audience until she was lacing up her boots.

"You're awful happy this morning," she said after getting a look at his face.

"Is it morning? I suppose that would explain the light through the window."

Moving her hands all the way to the top of her boots in a way that hiked her skirts up enough to show a good portion of her thigh, she asked, "Like that, do you?"

"Yes, ma'am."

"Well that's all you can have for now," she said while tightening the laces and letting her dress fall back down to cover them. "I've got matters to tend to."

"Before you go, I've got a question."

"If you're asking about me coming back, I'd say the odds are pretty good."

"That's fine, but not what I was going to ask. Where did you meet up with Edward Corrington?"

If she'd been mildly disappointed with not being the subject of the question, Jessica was positively dismayed when she heard what had really been on Slocum's mind. "I happened to meet Walter in New Orleans."

"You mean his editor, Walter Saunders?"

"That's right. I work in a little shop there that sells Eddie's books. I found out who Walter was and convinced him to introduce me to Eddie. Well, before you know it, I was invited along for a boat ride up the Mississippi for this traveling event of his."

Slocum sat up and swung his legs over the side of the bed. "Wait a second! You're telling me he's been spouting off about those books as far south as New Orleans?"

"It's all he talks about," she said. "He's very passionate."

"Since he's traveling with a harem of three women, I'd say so."

Jessica giggled and used a little silver comb to straighten

some of the more unruly sections of her hair. "Rose came in from Baton Rouge to meet Eddie, and Walter invited her to come along with us. She spends her nights with Walter and only pretends to worship Eddie when other folks can see. It's supposed to make him look like a big man. Hannah's just a little sweetie from Little Rock, innocent as you please. Eddie's had his sights set on her for a while, but those two are like a couple of puppies sniffing each other a bit before scampering away."

"You mean you and Edward haven't . . . ?"

"Not yet," she replied. "I've been closing in and meant to give Eddie something to write about while we were in Chicago. That part of the trip was canceled because Walter said there weren't a lot of sales coming from there."

"Thank God for small favors," Slocum grumbled.

Continuing to comb her hair while fretting with getting her dress just right, Jessica said, "Eddie's so shy. It was going to be delicious when I finally got him alone. Every now and then, he would touch my knee or say something as if he was the one getting ready to pounce. Precious."

"Have you ever seen a man named Michael Harper?"

"Sure," Jessica replied quickly enough to shock Slocum. "He showed up at most of the last bunch of Eddie's book parties. I even saw him sneaking in and out of this hotel."

"What did you say?"

She shrugged and stuck the comb in her hair so only the silver band could be seen. "He usually stays in the same place as Eddie. I don't think he wants to spook anyone, though, because he comes and goes so he's not noticed."

"But you noticed," Slocum pointed out.

"I notice a lot of things."

"Did you notice him shooting at us the other night?"

That caught her off guard, but Jessica was too composed to let it show as anything more than a flinch. "Certainly not. It doesn't surprise me, though. He always did have crazy eyes."

"And you didn't say anything when someone with crazy eyes showed up to meet Mr. Corrington?"

She chuckled and patted Slocum on the cheek. "You obviously haven't been to a lot of those parties. As far as last night goes, I didn't see much of anything apart from a whole lot of people running around like headless chickens as those shots went off. There was someone in a window, but that's all I could make out. It was so exciting!"

"Do you know what room he's in here?"

"Yes. I could get you in if you like."

Now it was Slocum's turn to be caught by surprise. "How?"

"I have a key that opens the doors to all the guest rooms."

"A skeleton key?"

"Yep. I convinced the man at the front desk to let me borrow it. Like I told you, I planned on giving Eddie a surprise, but then you came along." Looking him up and down like a hungry fox, she added, "I would have used it to get into this room, but I wasn't sure how you'd react. A man as dangerous as you is liable to do anything."

Slocum stepped up to her, wrapped his arms around her waist, and held her tightly. "You're quite a woman, Jessica."

"I know."

19

When Slocum made his way to the dining room, it was the time of day where late arrivals for breakfast were headed down, the early birds were on their way back up, hotel workers were cleaning up, and just about everyone else was carrying their bags to the lobby. Rather than fight all of that like a fish swimming upstream, Slocum sat down for breakfast. Most of the food had already been picked over, but there were enough biscuits and gravy left over to put a sizeable dent in his hunger. He was savoring his third cup of coffee when someone stomped into the dining room.

Sykes was in rough shape. His eye was blackened. His face was flushed and covered in fresh scrapes. There was even some dried blood along his hairline. He walked over to Slocum's table, noisily pulled out a chair, and dropped himself down onto it.

"You look like hell," Slocum said.

"I do, huh? You sit there sipping your fucking tea and point out that I look like hell. Well isn't that just fucking astute of you to notice?"

"Not tea," Slocum said. "It's coffee."

Sykes stared at him as if he was about to bust the table into pieces with his bare hands. Rather than give in to the fire that was obviously raging in him, he replied, "Proper *and* astute. What a delightful mix. Too bad you weren't observant enough to realize I turned up missing last night."

"To be honest, I was glad you didn't show up. I figured you'd heard that woman from Corrington's table last night wailing through the door and saved me the trouble of sending you away."

Despite the cuts, bumps, and bruises on his face, Sykes seemed genuinely intrigued when he asked, "Was it that sweet little blonde?"

"No. It was the one with the red hair."

"Good choice. While you were wrestling with her, I was getting ambushed by that pimp from Chicago. You know, the one you told me about?"

"James. What happened?"

"Him and that little prick partner of his jumped me when I was out surveying the local flavor."

"Which saloon did they find you at?" Slocum asked.

"Sadie's. It's two streets down. My intention was to spend the night away from that room so I could get some peace of mind. Well," Sykes added, "a piece of something. Know what I mean? So I was on my way and they jumped me. That little prick cracked me on the back of the head and the other one beat the tar out of me."

"Why wouldn't they just shoot you?"

Sykes straightened up and raised his eyebrows in an expression of pure horror. "Is that how you'd treat your partners?"

"No, but after the other night, I don't see why Harper would go through the trouble of tracking you down, laying an ambush, and seeing it through just to knock you around."

"Harper wasn't there," Sykes said. "This was just them other two. They knocked me around because they knew I was a friend of yours. Told me to deliver a message to you."

"Ahh. That makes more sense."

The waitress stopped by the table and smiled cheerily at Slocum. "Is there anything else I can get for you?" Although her eyes widened a bit when she got a look at Sykes, she didn't let it dim her smile.

"Since my friend is buying, I'll have steak and eggs, some potatoes, a bowl of grits, and some of that coffee."

When the waitress looked over to him, Slocum nodded.

"I'll round that up for you, sir."

"When that prick knocked me over the head, he took my gun," Sykes said after the waitress left. "I still ain't got it back!"

"What was the message you were supposed to deliver?"

"James said that if you fixed the damage you caused him in Chicago, he'd see to it that Harper left us alone."

Slocum laughed as if he was spitting each chuckle out like a hunk of rotten meat.

"Yeah," Sykes said. "That's pretty much what I thought. Even when I was dizzy after getting punched in the stomach I didn't believe that one. He did agree to set Harper up for us, though."

"That's still as long as I help him fix what happened in Chicago?"

"Yeah."

Slocum took a drink of coffee before telling him, "By that, James means put a bullet though my head in return for his friend getting killed. Or it could also mean getting me to Chicago and killing me there so everyone can see he's not some whipped dog that was chased away from its own home. You know that, right?"

"How the hell would I know that? I came up with something better than trusting either of them two."

"Oh, well that's good, I suppose."

"I say we go along as far as we need to go to get that bounty hunter off of our tails, clean up the situation with that writer, and then bury James and his little prick partner somewhere between here and Chicago. What do you say to that?"

Just as he was about to answer, Slocum focused his attention on the other side of the room. "Is that the little blonde from Corrington's supper table?"

Sykes turned around and nearly twisted himself out of his chair to get a look at Hannah sitting by herself at a table. At that same time, Slocum got a look at Sykes from a different angle. His hair was far from clean, but it sure didn't have the blood soaked into it that one might expect after getting hit hard enough to be put down. By the time Sykes turned back around, Slocum was taking another sip of coffee. "She's one pretty little thing, ain't she?" Sykes mused.

"Yes she is. So how are you supposed to let James know if you're going along with his plan?"

"They'll come by here to check on us."

"Will Harper be coming as well?"

"I don't see why he would," Sykes replied. "That'd go against the whole idea of the meeting."

"Not if the idea was to bring us into another trap. I've got to say this is a pretty sloppy attempt."

"Nobody said James or that other little prick was very smart."

"Not them," Slocum said. "I meant you."

Sykes was still glaring at him when the waitress returned with a cup of hot coffee and a bowl of warm grits. Sensing the tension in the air, she was quick to leave once her duty was done. Sykes picked up a spoon, stirred the melting butter into his grits, and then used that same spoon to stir his coffee.

"That's disgusting," Slocum said.

"It sure is. Accusing me of running some sort of plan after all we been through? You should be ashamed."

"Look at your coffee. There's grits floating in there now. Were you raised by wild animals?"

"Forget about what I eat, John. I don't like you talkin' to me that way."

"And I don't like some two-bit gunhand trying to set me up for another bunch of two-bit gunhands," Slocum replied. "That whole story you just told me was a joke and you know it. If you were going to go so far as to get your face bloodied, the least you could have done was get some sort of wound on the back of your head to go along with the rest of your account."

"You just think you're so smart, don't you?" Sykes said in a rumbling snarl. "You come up with one way of seeing something, so that's gotta be the only way there is. Well Edward Corrington came up with a way of lookin' at something and look where that got him. Here you go," he said while taking off his hat and slapping it onto the table. "Happy now?"

When Sykes twisted his head around, Slocum got a real good look at the blood crusted into his hair an inch or two above the groove made by his hat band.

"For your information," Sykes continued, "if I'd wanted to set you up for some sort of fall, I could've just told you to follow me into a dead-end alley for a drink. I've spent enough time riding with you to know you'd go anywhere if someone offered you a bottle of whiskey."

"All right. That's—"

Cutting Slocum off with a sharply upraised finger, Sykes told him, "Or I could have just knifed you in your sleep since you insisted on keeping me close enough to watch at all times. And as for the rest of your so-called opinions, I don't give a damn if there's some grits floating in my coffee. I happen to like the way the little bit of coffee on my spoon tastes when I eat my grits." To emphasize his point, Sykes scooped up some grits with his coffee-covered spoon and practically jammed them down his throat.

"You through?" Slocum asked.

"Hell no. I got a whole bowl left, plus my steak and eggs comin'."

"I meant with all your carrying on. Are you through with that?"

Reluctantly, Sykes muttered, "Yeah, I suppose so. I coulda saved myself a beating and handed you over right away."

"Or you could have not allowed yourself to get bush-whacked."

"Go to hell," Sykes snapped before stuffing another spoonful of grits into his mouth.

"Aww, don't be sore. I bought you breakfast, so maybe I could round up some flowers to go along with it. Would that make you feel better?"

Although Sykes's words couldn't be understood through the grits, their intent was easy enough to discern. Even with every syllable being garbled beyond recognition, the tone was angry enough to draw more than a few curious glances from other folks in the dining room.

"Sorry about that," Slocum said. "What do you think we should do about the men who jumped you?"

"Draw them out into the open and burn them down."

"Sounds simple enough. And Harper?"

Sykes tapped his spoon on his chin while contemplating. "Don't know yet. I think we might be able to deal with him rational."

"Falling back on reason, huh? That's a Gentleman Killer for you."

"Seems like Edward is more scared of Harper than we are. Maybe he could help us get the drop on him. He's been a slippery little cuss."

"That's just because we've been approaching him the wrong way." Shrugging, Slocum added, "All this time, I've treated him like a bounty hunter, and it turns out that he's just some loon trying to impress a writer. Worse yet, he thinks those books are fact because he's crazy. If it was just a mistake or an out-of-control rumor, I could wrap my head around it. Dealing with crazies is something else entirely."

"I dealt with plenty of them and you're right. There's no rhyme or reason. No way to predict what they're about to do."

"There's rhyme and reason," Slocum said. "We just need to start thinking like a crazy person."

Furrowing his brow, Sykes curled his lip and looked as if he'd bitten his tongue before finally admitting, "That ain't so easy."

"It may be if we can get a peek at whatever it is he's brought with him all this way while tagging along with Harper. We may even be able to get the drop on him for a change if we knew where to look."

As Slocum was speaking, the waitress returned with a plate of runny eggs and a cut of beef that was so rare it practically still had fur growing on it. Judging by how she set the plate in front of Sykes and hurried away, the server had been hoping to speed him out of the dining room as quickly as possible.

"What's her problem?" Sykes asked.

"You're an armed man covered in blood and spouting off like you're ready to flip this table over. What do you think her problem is?"

Sykes shrugged and cut into his steak. "Too bad we don't know where he's staying."

"I'll know pretty soon."

Stopping with his fork less than an inch from his mouth, Sykes asked, "You will? How?"

"From what I've heard, he's right here in this hotel." As he spoke, Slocum watched the lady who'd just entered the dining room.

Jessica strode up to his table, brushed a hand along his shoulder, and used the other to place a key in front of him. "Top of the steps," she whispered. "All the way to the right."

Her eyes lingered on Sykes's bloodied face, showing more than a little bit of interest before she smirked and walked away.

Picking up the key, Slocum said, "I was going to have a look in his room myself, but was waiting for a chance to get in there without being seen by all the folks coming and going right now."

"Seems to be quiet now," Sykes said. "Mind if I come along?"

"Actually, I may need you to act as a lookout."

"Great!" Although he started to get up, Sykes quickly sat down again. "Can I finish my steak first?"

20

Harper's room was at the end of the second floor hallway that faced the street. It was a prime spot for a man to keep his back to a wall, have everyone else where he could see them, and maintain a vantage point from high ground. The only thing wrong with it was that it was a stone's throw away from the men he was stalking. Harper had to know Slocum was staying at that hotel, but was bold enough to stay close anyway. Or perhaps that's where the crazy part came in.

On the other hand, this could still be some sort of ruse to get Slocum to take a wrong step that would end up with him playing into someone's hands. When he thought back to how this whole mess had started, Slocum cursed himself for thinking too damn much. Corrington was just a writer who'd used the wrong man's name to sell his books. James and Cam were just pimps and crooks who had a score to settle. Sykes needed to make sure more zeroes weren't added to the price that was already on his head, and Harper was just a maniac trying to impress his idol. Once Slocum had pulled all those strings apart, he saw they didn't actually form one solid length of rope. They were just a bunch of loose ends that needed tying.

Slocum checked over his shoulder as he approached the door. Sykes was at the opposite end of the hall, in a corner marked by a pair of small doors that looked like they led to a closet. He wasn't as far from the stairs as Slocum was now, but he could watch the staircase and most of the rest of the second floor without being easily spotted himself. Probably still picking the steak from his teeth, Sykes gave him a wave to let Slocum know everything was good on his end.

Slocum didn't trust that man completely, but he figured their arrangement was still mutually beneficial enough for them to work together. And if Sykes planned on double-crossing him, he already would have taken a shot using the holdout pistol Slocum had loaned him. The sooner that shoe was dropped, the quicker one loose end would be cut.

Fishing the skeleton key from his pocket, Slocum eased it into the lock and slowly turned it. He kept one hand on the door handle and held his breath. There was no way of knowing for certain if Jessica had been truthful with him. After all, he'd already been betrayed by one woman on this hunt. Even if Jessica's intentions were good, there was no way of knowing if Harper was in his room at that moment. For that matter, Slocum didn't know if his footsteps had been heard and Harper already had a gun pointed at the door.

Every little click within the lock mechanism sounded like a gunshot in his ears.

When the lock clicked for the last time, Slocum swore the entire door shook within its frame.

Pushing the door open slowly produced a grating creak from the hinges, so Slocum just shoved it open and was done with it. What he found inside was more than just a loose end. It was the hand that had been fraying the entire rope.

"What the hell is this?" Slocum asked when he saw Harper leaning against the wall near his window and Corrington sitting at a small desk against the wall adjacent to the door.

Harper straightened up and reflexively reached for the gun at his side, but stopped short when Slocum's hand slapped firmly against the grip of his Colt Navy.

Corrington raised both arms as if he was being robbed for the pencil and paper in his grasp. "This isn't what you think! I merely discovered Mr. Harper was right down the hall from me and decided to pay him a visit. You know, to help ease the tensions between us all."

Walking over to the desk without taking his eyes off of Harper, Slocum said, "Then you won't mind letting me take a gander at what you're writing."

"There's no need. I was simply signing a book."

"That's not a book you were writing in," Slocum pointed out.

"Not a finished book, no," Corrington sputtered. "It's a work in progress. A manuscript. I thought Mike might like to read it over before it's released for the public's approval."

"If it's anything like the rest of your books," Slocum said, "there's already a bunch of folks in the public that won't approve." Now that he was close enough to the desk to see the papers in front of the writer, Slocum spread out the small stack so he could glance at them. From what he could tell, they were hastily scribbled notes detailing some very familiar instances. "Is this about the times me and Harper locked horns the other night?"

The writer looked like he was ready to try and squirm out of his skin. "I was having a conversation with Mr. Harper," he explained. "I meant to try and resolve all of this, but—"

"Don't give me that bullshit," Slocum said as he turned toward Corrington. "You mean to write about the times when me and him traded shots. Either one of us could have been killed! Doesn't that bother you in the slightest?"

Corrington stammered a few syllables, but didn't get a chance to say much else before Harper went for his gun.

It happened in a flicker of movement that Slocum almost missed. In his burst of anger at what was going on, Slocum had taken his eyes away from his main target. As soon as he saw Harper twitch, he drew his Colt.

Harper was faster than Slocum had expected, but not very accurate. He cleared leather before Slocum, pulled his trigger, and sent a shot hissing past Slocum's ear.

Cool under fire, Slocum drew his Colt and fired as Corrington rammed into him from the side to knock off his aim. Swearing under his breath, Slocum wasn't about to make the same mistake twice. He kept his eyes fixed on Harper even as he reached across with his left hand to grab Corrington by the shirt and throw him to the floor. "Stay down if you know what's good for you!" he shouted to the writer.

Harper fired a few more times in quick succession, filling the room with hot lead.

Slocum's response was to stay low and pick his shot. He squeezed his trigger and grazed the other man's side. Harper clutched at the wound while firing the rest of his shots at Slocum. Fortunately, the room had also filled with acrid smoke, which marred his vision and burned his eyes enough to make all of his shots near misses. Unfortunately, Slocum didn't have much better luck and fired two misguided shots into the wall as Harper scrambled for cover.

"Stop this!" Corrington shouted as he clawed at Slocum's leg. "There's no need for all of this blood! I can fix things!"

"You've done enough!" Slocum said.

When he heard the door swing open, Slocum thought the writer had found a way to skitter across the floor and work the handle himself. He'd just lined up a shot at Harper's skull when Slocum felt a set of thick hands drop down on his shoulders and pull him out into the hall. The next thing he felt was the wall pounding against his spine hard enough to cause his fist to clench and send a shot into the floor.

When Slocum was pounded against the wall a second time, the impact knocked the gun from his hand.

"So you came to us, huh?" James said as he peeled Slocum off the wall and snapped his fist into his face. "Saves us a bit of trouble."

Slocum pushed away from the wall, which gave him just enough space to snap his leg back and drive it straight up into James's groin. His boot thumped against some very delicate parts of the other man's anatomy, loosening James's grip so Slocum could pull completely away. Less than a second after he moved, a bullet from Harper's gun knocked a hole through the spot where Slocum's head had been.

If he'd been keeping track of the number of shots fired, that information had been knocked out of Slocum's head when he was slammed against the wall. Rather than take his chances that Harper's cylinder was dry, Slocum grabbed James's shirt and shoved him farther down the hall. But they weren't the only ones filling the hall with the sounds of a struggle. At the far end, Sykes was in an all-out brawl with another man. He delivered a solid uppercut to the man's chin, spinning him around enough for Slocum to get a look at Cam's face.

"Been waitin' for this for a while," James said as he charged at Slocum. The problem with kicking a man south of the border was that he was madder than hell when his eyesight cleared up from the initial blow. James was so fired up now that he nearly put his fist through the wall when Slocum stepped aside to clear a path for the incoming punch.

While he was in the vicinity, Slocum drove a few punches of his own into James's ribs. The other man was too angry to feel them and needed a lot more punishment than that to slow him down. Slocum lashed out with as many punches as he could, hoping they might be enough to chop James down like a tree.

"Get out of my way!" Harper shouted from within the next room. Corrington's voice followed that in a wave of nervous chatter. Slocum couldn't make out the words, but he saw that the writer was clinging to the other man in a similar fashion to how he'd weighed Slocum down earlier.

A solid fist delivered to Slocum's stomach doubled him over and forced him to hack up a pained breath. "That's what I like to hear!" James said. "Shouldn't have wronged me in Chicago. Now you gotta pay!" He immediately made good on his threat by hitting Slocum again in the same spot.

When that second punch landed, Slocum thought he might pass out. If that happened, he knew he probably wouldn't wake up again. It was pure force of will that got him to stand up straight, pull in a breath, and fight back. Putting all the strength he could muster behind a punch intended for James's chin, he wound up scraping his knuckles against James's chest instead.

James smiled as if he'd just gotten an early Christmas gift. Clamping a hand around Slocum's throat, he knocked his head against a wall and leaned in to tell him, "Think I'll drag your carcass all the way back to Chicago. After that, maybe I can write about how it feels to be the man who killed John Sl—"

When Slocum snapped his head forward, his forehead cracked against James's nose. The rest of the boast wound up lodged in the back of James's throat along with a few teeth and a surprised yelp of pain. Unfortunately, the head-butt hurt Slocum only slightly less. When he turned to get a look down the hall to check on Sykes, Slocum felt dizzy enough to lose his footing. His back touched the wall and he used it for support, but he still felt as if he could fold at any second.

"Son of a bitch!" James roared as he pressed one hand to his face. With his other hand, he made a clumsy reach for his pistol. Blood poured from the wound that had been put there when Slocum had cracked him in Chicago. That wound, combined with all the others, threw off James's aim enough so his bullet landed several feet off target.

Hearing the shot echo in such close proximity caused Slocum's entire body to react. He dove for his Colt and fired back. To call that shot wild would have been generous, but it did a good enough job of getting James away from him. When he squeezed his trigger again, Slocum heard only the metallic slap of the hammer against empty brass.

Suddenly, Corrington bolted from the room. He carried a .32 in one hand as if he hardly knew which end of a gun to hold. "I've disarmed Mr. Harper and now I'll see to it that you men stop as well! I won't have anyone hurt on my account!"

Harper stepped into the doorway next. As soon as he spotted Slocum, he drew his .32 from the holster under his arm.

Slocum rammed his shoulder into the closest door he could find and stampeded inside as the .32 was fired behind him in a quick series of pops. His ears were ringing from the noise and his head was still jangling from the head-butt as he reloaded his Colt. Someone hurried toward the room as Slocum finished putting the third round in the cylinder. That would have to be good enough.

He approached the door and was immediately overwhelmed by the mass of James's body. The gunman must have been gambling on the fact that Slocum was still off his game, because he charged in like he'd been invited. A wide, predatory smile was on his face as he once again grabbed Slocum's throat.

"This time I'm wringin' yer goddamn neck," James said as his grip tightened.

Slocum felt his balance waver and his eyesight dim. The thump of his own heartbeat filled his ears so much that he barely heard the shot when he jammed the Colt's barrel into the other man's belly and pulled his trigger.

James bucked, but his grip remained strong. His eyes

showed more confusion than anything else as he grunted, "You shot me?"

Slocum had to finish the job he'd started before James choked the life from him and dragged him down into hell along with him. With Harper surely coming for him, Slocum couldn't allow himself to be pinned down like a lamb staked out for the lions. Harper had already proven himself to be just the sort of man to take advantage of that situation. Cursing James for making him waste the second of his three bullets, Slocum angled the Colt upward and pulled his trigger again.

This time, the bullet sent a jolt through James's entire body. No longer stunned, the gunman threw both arms out to his sides and staggered back. He turned on one heel, pivoted around to show Slocum the messy holes that had been blown through his torso, and dropped.

Someone in the room screamed, causing Slocum to spin around and take aim with his pistol. He recognized the brunette who had been sitting at Corrington's table along with Walter and the other two women; he hadn't realized it was her room he'd busted into.

"Sorry, ma'am," he said, "but you might want to hide somewhere until the shooting stops."

Rose didn't need to hear any more than that before she scooted off the far side of the bed and huddled with it between her and the door.

"You've got to listen to me, John . . . Good Lord!" Corrington exclaimed when he rushed in and nearly tripped over James's corpse.

Slocum meant to throw the writer somewhere he wouldn't get shot, but the fire in Slocum's eyes was more than enough to send Corrington into a panic.

"I'm sorry, John! Please don't kill me!" he wailed as he backed into the hall.

Before Slocum could do or say anything to warn him,

the writer was grabbed from behind by Harper and held in place to act as a shield.

As more gunshots were fired back and forth at the end of the hall, Harper twitched nervously while holding his .32 against the writer's temple. "You wanted a good end to your series about real gunmen," he said. "Looks to me like we're about to write one together."

"This isn't what I wanted," Corrington insisted.

"Isn't it?" Slocum asked. "From what I saw, you and him were having a nice little chat. Makes sense to me. You send some fancy-dressed back-shooter to kick up some dust and then write about it. Sells a lot of books!"

"No, he was only a consultant," Corrington insisted. "He had some good stories to share and I embellished upon them. That's all it was supposed to be."

"You know what he's been doing," Slocum said. "You told me and Dan all about it." Shifting his gaze to the man directly behind the writer, he added, "In fact, Mike, he told us that you were one of the craziest men he'd ever met."

"He wouldn't do that!" Harper said.

"I'm not so sure. Why don't you ask him?"

Cinching his arm in a bit tighter around Corrington's neck, Harper asked, "Is that true? Did you tell these men I was crazy so they would kill me?"

Corrington's face was turning from flushed pink to dark red. "You . . . threatened to shoot me that time. Remember?"

"Only because you didn't want to list my name in your next book."

"I never told you to go after anyone," the writer croaked. "I just thought you were a bounty hunter with some good stories."

"I told you about how I found out where John Slocum really was. Then I told you about what happened in Chicago."

"You did?" Slocum growled.

Corrington winced and struggled to draw a breath. "Books were . . . selling. I'm just a . . . just a writer."

"And," Slocum said, "if your next book just happened to be the first to give a written account of the last days of someone like me or Sykes, well that would probably sell quicker than cups of cold water in hell. Ain't that the idea?"

Even though Harper was the one squashing his head like a grape, Corrington appeared to be more afraid of Slocum. When he spoke this time, it was more of a squeak. "You don't . . . understand just how . . . how well those books sold."

"Go ahead, Harper. Pull his head off."

"Set your gun down or his blood truly will be on your hands," Harper replied.

Slocum lowered his arm and let it hang limply from his shoulder. "Then what? You let him go and shoot me anyway?"

"You've got to pay for what you done in Fort Griffin, John. You can either take your punishment like a man or you can be put down like a dog."

"I didn't slaughter any eight folks in Fort Griffin, you crazy bastard!"

"I'm not crazy!"

But his eyes told a different story. When Slocum looked into them, he could see a storm raging inside of Michael Harper that couldn't be found inside a man that had his head screwed on tight. Even though he was staring at Slocum, Harper didn't appear to be seeing much of anything at all. His lips trembled with words that were flowing in his mind but which he was unable to say. Hands shook as knuckles whitened. Sweat dripped from his brow with the strain of dealing with whatever demons had brought him to the conclusion that Corrington's cheap novels were gospel.

"Fine," Slocum sighed. "You win. If you swear I'll see a judge, I'll take my chances with him."

Harper nodded and released his grip on Corrington.

"Edward," Slocum said, "MOVE!"

The writer dropped straight down as Slocum snapped his arm up like a whip and fired at the point when it would have cracked.

Backing toward the door, Harper fired his .32. His shots thumped into the bed, but Slocum's had already dug a messy hole through his chest. As Harper stumbled into the hall, the crazy fire in him burned brightly enough for him to raise his gun again. Even worse than that: Slocum's Colt was empty.

"You're done, John," Harper said as he used his last bit of strength to take aim.

In a whisper of something cutting through the air followed by the wet thump of a blade sinking home, Harper's last bit of strength was taken from him. He no longer had enough steam to lift his arm or remain on his feet. Blood sprayed from the side of his neck and he crumpled.

Sykes walked up to Harper's body and pried the pocketknife from where it had been lodged. "See why I had to have this back at that store?" he said as he wiped it clean upon Harper's shirt. "You hardly ever find one that's balanced good enough for throwin'."

Rose peeked up from behind the bed, saw the carnage in her room as well as the body in the hallway, and screamed.

Corrington either didn't have the strength or the will to get to his feet, so he merely crawled over to Slocum and gazed up at him. "I never knew Mike would truly go after you like that. He came to me with some interesting ideas, ways to make a character that would hunt your characters down in future books. It would tie all of my works together! It wasn't supposed to actually happen."

"But even when you found out it did happen, you were going to write about it anyway," Slocum said.

"What else was I to do?" Looking over to Sykes, Corrington pleaded, "I told you Mike was crazy. I told you he wouldn't leave me alone."

When Sykes looked over to him, Slocum said, "I found this one and Harper having a friendly chat together. Seems they were plotting the next book."

"Is that so?"

"What happened to you?"

"Them two from Chicago came storming up the stairs when the ruckus started. The big fella got ahead of me, but I wasn't about to let the other one tip the scales even more." Looking back to Corrington, Sykes said, "Had a little chat with him. Turned out about the same as the chat with Harper over there."

Corrington shuddered as he thought about what condition Cam could possibly be in. "I'll make this up to you men, I swear."

"Damn right you will," Sykes said as he lunged at the writer with the same knife he'd just pulled from another man's neck. "Whatever money you make offa them books that use me and John's name, we get a cut of it. *Comprendes?*"

"Sure. I can arrange a payment tomorrow."

"And you'll set the records straight about us," Sykes added.

"Naturally."

"And whenever you get a dime from any of them books later on, or money from any other books you write that's got anything to do with anyone that so much as has a passing resemblance to me or John, we get a cut. If some bastard you write about carries a gun, that's close enough. We don't get our cut, and we come for you. Or," Sykes added as he held the blade out so Corrington could see the way it caught the light, "maybe just *I'll* come see you."

Corrington clawed at the bed to help drag himself to his feet. "That's preposterous! This wasn't *all* my fault! You can't seriously expect me to abide by that agreement! Mr. Slocum is a man of honor and reason. Surely he can agree to something more feasible."

All this time, Slocum had been reloading his Colt. Downstairs, folks were in an uproar about the fight that had taken place. The law was surely on their way, but none of that registered on Slocum's face. He was cold as could be when he rolled the Colt's cylinder against his palm and said, "I don't know, Mr. Corrington. My partner's proposal seems plenty agreeable."

21

NEW ORLEANS
TWO MONTHS LATER

Slocum didn't need much of an excuse to spend some time in New Orleans. Considering how cold it was getting up north, the southern climate was much more tolerable anyhow. This time, however, he had better reason than usual to sit in a little café that smelled of gumbo and watch a pretty woman approach him.

"Here you go," Jessica said as she sat down at his table and placed a fat envelope in front of him.

He opened the envelope just enough to see the cash inside, then stuck it in his jacket pocket and asked, "Did Sykes get his share?"

"And then some, just like you. Aren't you going to count it?"

"No. That writer was too scared to cheat us."

Unable to contain herself, Jessica said, "It's a lot. Those books are doing really well."

"Good."

186

"And so is the new one."

Slocum didn't have anything to say to that.

Jessica said, "I have a copy of the new book. See for yourself."

She handed Slocum another novel with another fanciful drawing on the cover. This time, there was a lone man holding a gun in each hand standing on top of a riverboat that was sailing through what looked like a sea of dead bodies.

"Jesus," Slocum grumbled. "People really pay for this?"

"That's you on there," she announced.

Holding the cover closer, he was able to see no familiar features on the man standing beneath the title, *King of the River*. "Sure don't look like me."

"Well it is. You're mentioned by name."

Pulling the book open almost hard enough to shred it, Slocum found his name on the third page—and damn near every one after that. "Son of a bitch!"

"You're the hero, John," Jessica said, while patting his knee. "Acquitted of all crimes and back to bestow righteous vengeance upon those who wronged you. He talks you up better in here than when the law came to ask him who started shooting in Perryville."

"What about Sykes?"

"He's in there too. Just not as big of a hero."

"Figures. You've read this, haven't you?"

Nodding, she replied, "Oh yes."

Slocum felt the color rushing into his face.

"Don't be embarrassed," she told him. "I liked it." As her hand slipped up along his thigh to rub his groin under cover of the tablecloth, she whispered, "Let's go somewhere else so I can show you just how much I liked it."

More than willing to forget about the gumbo he'd ordered, Slocum tossed his napkin onto the table and escorted Jessica out of the café. "It's good to be king."

Watch for

SLOCUM AND THE DIRTY DOZEN

380th novel in the exciting SLOCUM series
from Jove

Coming in October!